When I Hit You

Meena Kandasamy is a poet, fiction writer, translator and activist who lives in Chennai and London. She has published two collections of poetry, *Touch* and *Ms Militancy*, and the critically acclaimed novel, *The Gypsy Goddess*, which was longlisted for the Dylan Thomas Prize and the DSC Prize in 2015.

When I Hit You

MEENA KANDASAMY

 Atlantic Books • LONDON

First published in hardback in Great Britain in 2017
by Atlantic Books, an imprint of Atlantic Books Ltd.

This paperback edition published in Great Britain
in 2018 by Atlantic Books.

10 9 8 7 6 5 4 3 2

A CIP catalogue record for this book is available from the British Library.

Paperback ISBN: 978 1 78649 128 2
E-book ISBN: 978 1 78649 127 5

Printed and bound in Great Britain by Clays Ltd, St Ives plc

Atlantic Books
An imprint of Atlantic Books Ltd
Ormond House
26–27 Boswell Street
London WC1N 3JZ

www.atlantic-books.co.uk

To Cedric,
and Amma, Appa and Thenral

I

This is about the future of her only daughter, really the only thing that matters to her in life, the only reason for her late nights and efforts, in short, her only hope, her only consolation, and she is not going to sit on her hands watching her throw her life in the garbage.

PILAR QUINTANA,
COLECCTIONISTAS DE POLVOS RAROS

My mother has not stopped talking about it.

Five years have passed, and with each year, her story has mutated and transformed, most of the particulars forgotten, the sequence of events, the date of the month, the day of the week, the time of the year, the etcetera and the so on, until only the most absurd details remain.

So, when she begins to talk about the time that I ran away from my marriage because I was being routinely beaten and it had become unbearable and untenable for me to keep playing the role of the good Indian wife, she does not talk about the monster who was my husband, she does not talk about the violence, she does not even talk about the actual chain of events that led to my running away. That is not the kind of story you will be getting out of my mother, because my mother is a teacher, and a teacher knows that there is no reason to state the obvious. As a teacher, she also knows that to state the obvious is, in fact, a sure sign of stupidity.

When she tells the story of my escape, she talks of my feet. (Even when I'm around. Even when my feet are actually visible to her audience. Even when my toes curl in shame. Even when the truth is that my feet had no role in my escape, except to carry me a hundred yards at the most to the nearest

auto-rickshaw. My mother seems oblivious to my embarrass-
ment. In fact, I suspect she quite enjoys the spectacle.)

'You should have seen her feet,' she says. 'Were they even
feet? Were they the feet of my daughter? No! Her heels were
cracked and her soles were twenty-five shades darker than
the rest of her, and with one look at the state of her slippers
you could tell that she did nothing but housework all the
time. They were the feet of a slave.'

And then she beats her rounded mouth with her four
fingers together and makes this sound that goes O O O O O.
It is meant to convey that what happened was lamentable –
indeed, should not really have happened at all. This is also
the way Tamil mothers beat their mouths when they hear of
the death of a cousin's acquaintance by misadventure or the
neighbour's daughter's elopement – signifying the appropriate mix of sadness and shock, and, most importantly,
disapproval.

Sometimes, when she is in a more relaxed mood, and
feeling flush with tenderness for her husband of thirty-six
years, she will say something along the lines of: 'He is such
a devoted father. You remember the time we had that trouble, and my daughter came back to us, with her feet looking
like a prisoner's, all blackened and cracked and scarred and
dirt an inch thick around every toenail? He washed her feet
with his own hands, scrubbing and scrubbing and scrubbing
them with hot water and salt and soap and an old toothbrush

and applying cream and baby oil to clean and soften them. He would cry to me afterward. If this is the state of her feet, what must she have endured inside her? Her broken marriage broke my husband, too.' But that is the kind of thing that she says only to close relatives, to family friends, and the few remaining people who are still cordial to her even though she has a runaway daughter at home. That is about six and a half people in all of Chennai.

She does not stay on the subject of my feet for long, because what more can she say about it, especially to an audience of semi-elderly people with a laundry list of *actual* health complaints? The story of the feet is a story that does not travel far. They are useful but limited metaphors. It is the other story, the story set at the other extremity of my body – of what happened to my hair, and, more specifically, my mother's rescue mission – that gets more publicity. It is this story that she insinuates into every conversation, hoping that the stranger across from her will press her for more details. The potent combination of medical advice, cautionary tale and lived experience is irresistible to her borderline hypochondriac friends, and she unfailingly plays her role with style. Over the years, she has emerged as some kind of faith-healer in her friends' circle, largely because she has managed to preserve herself into her sixties in a more or less pristine form.

'Stress. Stress can have any reaction on the body. Stress is what's making your psoriasis worse. Skin and hair. That's the first level where stress operates. When my daughter was having a bad time – yes, in that marriage – you cannot imagine what happened to her hair. What can I say? Distance yourself from the stress. Do breathing exercises. Learn to be relaxed.'

Or:

'It is just stress. When one is stressed, one loses one's immunity completely. The body's defence mechanism is broken. It is a free-for-all situation. You are catching colds all the time because of stress. Don't laugh now. When my daughter was with that bastard, married and gone away, she was under so much stress that when she returned it took me months to get her back to normal. She was brittle and empty like a shell. Any disease could have snatched her away from us. It sounds unlikely to you, especially when you see her like this, but you really cannot imagine. Ask me about it. Even her hair was not spared. It was *teeming*. That's an epic in itself.'

Or:

'[Insert name of a chronic condition] is nothing, nothing that care and love cannot solve. The cure is not even in medicine. It is in the state of mind. You have to stop worrying. Every day after that is a day of progress. Worry just kills you from the inside. Any disease can take hold of you. I've seen that in my daughter's case. God, her hair! But every problem, every condition can be fought, and it can be vanquished.'

And in the extremely unlikely event that this constant, direct reference has not sparked sufficient interest in the listener for her to divulge my follicle 'condition', she would move on briskly and disapprovingly to talk about other things. In most cases, however, the recipient of her token advice always seemed to have a healthy curiosity, and this pleased her enormously.

'I have never seen so much lice in my life. Lice, or louse, or however you call it. You know what I'm talking about. Her hair was swarming with it. She would be sitting by my side and I could see these creatures run across her head. They would drop on her shoulder. I put her through twelve years of school and she had hair that reached her knees and not once did she have any problem with head lice. Not once. Now, she was back home after only four months of marriage, and that criminal had cut my daughter's hair short, and it was in–fes–ted. The lice drained my girl of all energy. I would put a white bedsheet over her head and rub her hair and then the sheet would be full of lice. At least a hundred. Killing them individually was impossible, so I'd dunk the sheet in boiling water. I tried shampoo, *sheekakaai*, Nizoral and neem leaves – nothing worked.'

With each progressive retelling, the hundreds became thousands, the thousands tended towards infinity, and the lice multiplied, becoming settlements and then townships and then cities and then nations. In my mother's version of the story, these lice caused traffic disturbances on my hair, they took evening walks on my slender neck, they had civil war over territory, they recruited an enormous number of overenthusiastic child soldiers and then they engaged in out-and-out war with my mother. They mounted organized resistance, set up base camps in the soft area of the scalp above the ears and in the nape of the neck where it was always harder to reach, but they were being decimated slowly and surely by my mother's indefatigable efforts. Every war strategy was deployed, Sun Tzu was invoked: appear weak when you are strong and appear strong when you are weak; when your opponent is of choleric temper, seek to irritate him with more chlorinated washes than he can handle; attack him when he is unprepared; force your enemy to reveal himself; be as rapid as the wind when you are wielding the *paenseeppu* (the merciless narrow-toothed lice comb that removed as many hairs as it removed lice and lice eggs and baby lice); make use of the sun and the strongest shampoo; above all, do not spend time bothering about lice rights and genocide tribunals when you are defending a liberated zone.

This is how my story of Young Woman as a Runaway Daughter became, in effect, the great battle of My Mother versus the Head Lice. And because my mother won this battle, the story was told endlessly, and it soon entered the canon of literature on domestic violence. The Americans had trigger warnings and graphic-content cautions attached to the course material, but otherwise it picked up a lot of traction elsewhere. It was taught in gender studies programmes, and women of colour discussed it in their reading groups (it was still a little too dirty and disorienting for white feminists, and it was perhaps considered a touch too environmentally unfriendly for the ecofeminists, and the postmodernists disregarded it because my mother's telling ignored the crucial concept of my husband's agency to beat me), and even those who forgot the original context of the story or the bad-marriage setting always remembered it as a fable about one mother's unending, unconditional, over conditioned love.

* *

Naturally, I hope that anyone can understand why I am reluctant to allow my mother's story to become the Standard, Authorized, King James Version of my misadventures in marriage.

Much as I love my mother, authorship is a trait that I have come to take *very* seriously. It gets on my nerves when she steals the story of my life and builds her anecdotes around it. It's plain plagiarism. It also takes a lot of balls to do something like that – she's stealing from a writer's life – how often is that sort of atrocity even *allowed* to happen? The number one lesson I have learnt as a writer: *Don't let people remove you from your own story.* Be ruthless, even if it is your own mother.

If I do not act immediately, I fear that her engaging narrative may override the truth. It will damn me for eternity because every reference to the sad tale of my marriage will be indexed under: Head Louse, Ectoparasite, *Pediculus humanus capitis*.

I need to stop this, before my story becomes a footnote to a story about lice infestation.

I must take some responsibility over my own life.

I must write my story.

II

Life While-You-Wait.
Performance without rehearsal.
Body without alterations.
Head without premeditation.

I know nothing of the role I play.
I only know it's mine. I can't exchange it.

I have to guess on the spot
just what this play's all about.

Ill-prepared for the privilege of living,
I can barely keep up with the pace that the action
*   demands.*
I improvise, although I loathe improvisation.

WISLAWA SZYMBORSKA, 'LIFE WHILE-YOU-WAIT'

There are not many things a woman can become when she is a housewife in a strange town that does not speak any of her mother-tongues. Not when her life revolves around her husband. Not when she has been trapped for two months in the space of three rooms and a veranda.

Primrose Villa, with its little walled garden, its two side entrances, has the quaint air of kept secrets. It is the sort of setting that demands drama. The white and magenta bougainvillea creepers in their lush September bloom. Papaya plants, along the east wall, with their spiralling, umbrella leaves and frail trunks. A coconut tree in its advanced years, its leaves designed to frame the solitary moon at night and play an air-piano in the rain.

Fifty yards away squats the home of the nearest neighbour, who collects the rent from us on behalf of his landlord-brother. On the other side, a second entrance to the house opens up on to a little alley that turns into a narrow cobbled path and leads to a nuns' cloister and a cemetery. In the middle of this, the house itself stands, small and self-contained, its well-defined boundaries in sharp contrast to the open, vibrant garden.

It makes a perfect film set. And in some ways, that is

how I think of it: it is easier to imagine this life in which I'm trapped as a film; it is easier when I imagine myself as a character. It makes everything around me appear less frightening; my experiences at a remove. Less painful, less permanent. Here, long before I ever faced a camera, I became an actress.

One has to enter our home through a moaning wooden door, once upon a time painted teal. Inside, there is an excuse for a living room with two red plastic chairs and a table, on which I've arranged the rice-cooker and the mixie and the iron and a stack of all of today's newspapers. On the wall beside this table, a calendar from my husband's college. This is the room that opens into every other space in the house. To its left, the kitchen countertop with the shiny utensils and a gas stove; underneath it, the standard-issue red gas cylinder; above it, tiny maroon-framed windows that look into the garden, scissors and tea filters hanging from hooks on the wall, a sink in the corner where only one person can stand, a brand new fridge that seems out of place. Step into the next room, and there is our bedroom that overlooks the road, its windows covered in thick ochre and rust-red curtains that I cannot be bothered to change and a large plywood bed that creaks. Of course, the bathroom with its white tiles and scuttling cockroaches and a big blue barrel to hold water. Next, a dungeon-room that smells of damp and dread where we keep our clothes, our books, and assorted furniture left behind by an owner who lacked the heart or the care to throw things away. What else? The walls covered in coats of a yellow lime that swells in the rains like an expectant mother. On these sun-bleached walls, squares of deep colour where pictures were once hung, now framing rich blankness. Red oxide floors that need to be swept and mopped every evening. Lizards as still and ancient as the house. Rats that announce their presence only at night. This is the space within which I must move.

Everything here must be left looking as untouched as possible for the sake of continuity. Every object must be put back precisely where it belonged. This is not only because my husband loses his temper about misplacement, but because no one who watches a film expects objects to be jumping around from one frame to the next. Objects do not have legs of their own to get up and walk away. That being the unfortunate truth, it becomes my fault when they are out of place and my responsibility to return them to their respective positions.

It is only one of the expectations I must consider in my role as a perfect wife. The most important, of course, as an act*ress*, is how I look.

Here, there is more to undo than to do. I begin by wearing my hair the way he wants it: gathered and tamed into a ponytail, oiled, sleek, with no sign of disobedience. I skip the kohl around my eyes because he believes that it is worn only by screen-sirens and seductresses. I wear a dull T-shirt and pajama-bottoms because he approves of dowdiness.

Or, I wrap myself in an old cotton sari to remind me of my mother. Some days, when I am especially eager to impress and to escape punishment, I slip into the shapeless monstrosity that is: *the nightie.*

The effect of adhering to my husband's wishes gives me the appearance of a woman who has given up. But, I know that attired in this manner, I am all set to play the part of the good housewife. Nothing loud, nothing eye-catching, nothing beautiful. I should look like a woman whom no one wants to look at or, more accurately, whom no one even sees.

I should be a blank. With everything that reflects my personality cleared out. Like a house after a robbery. Like a mannequin stripped of its little black dress and dragged away from the store window, covered in a bedsheet and locked off in the godown.

This is the plainness that makes him pleased. This plainness that has peeled away all my essence, a plainness that can be controlled and moulded to his will. This is the plainness that I will wear today, this plain mask on a pretty face, this plainness that will hide me, this plainness that will prevent arguments.

* *

Plainness is its own protection. Sometimes, those who seek to protect something go one step further, dragging plainness down to the level of ugliness.

When I was a baby, my mother would powder me and put a big black dot of kohl on both my cheeks, to keep away the evil eye. She continued doing it through primary school. I think I would not have suffered as much from the anticipated evil eye as I did from the taunts of my classmates.

My father has a small black tattoo, the size of a peppercorn, right in the middle of his forehead. When my grandmother gave birth to him after fourteen years of self-imposed child-lessness, the boy-child was so beautiful that she believed the gods would be tempted to take him back. To prevent any attempts of the divinity to reclaim her son, she made him im-perfect. He was spared. Over the last sixty years, that gypsy tattoo has faded into a pale green.

I do not have to go that far. I use this mask of plainness to ward off suspicions in my husband's mind. This plainness comforts him greatly because it renders me unattractive to the world around me. The situation has not yet deteriorat-ed to the point where I have to take recourse in disfiguring myself. For the moment, this will do.

* *

Lights, camera, action.

Rolling, rolling, role-playing.

Ext. It is early evening. She stands at the threshold of the house, waiting for him. Her right shoulder against the door frame. The gaze into the distance. The restlessness captured in her left foot tracing circles on the floor. On an impulse, she decides to step forward and walks out of their garden and waits for him on the street. There is an element of nervous excitement about her that renders even her plainness becoming. She hesitates. She is still. She moves again, afraid to be spotted on the street, afraid of staying there, she retraces her steps hurriedly and waits for him by the door. She takes the same position as before. Leaning on the frame. Staring at the garden. When she spots his quick, wiry figure against the horizon, she runs obediently to him. Not a real run, but a semi-run that would meet his approval. Most importantly, not a run where her breasts jounce and jiggle as if to proclaim their existence.

She stretches up on tiptoes to kiss his cheek and they walk back together, shutting the door behind them.

Int. She takes his bag from his shoulders and deposits it carefully on a shelf. She looks at him, smiles, holds herself in that position for a few seconds, and then hurries to the fridge to pour a glass of orange juice. She remembers to wipe the condensation from the glass with the hem of her shirt. She kisses him, almost reverentially, on the neck. She pulls back, smiles. What follows is his reciprocal kiss, a hug, a clumsy grabbing. She is still smiling. Everything about her radiates the happiness of receiving her husband who has returned home after a long day at work.

Now, when the action has fallen into place, it is the time for dialogue, the time to reel off her well-rehearsed lines.

She asks him how his day at the college was. She keeps talking as he undresses, keeps talking as she wads his clothes in the washing basket. She tells him that she missed him. She asks him if he has papers to grade. She talks of how she was reading Lenin, or Mao, or Samir Amin (or some other ancient Communist dignitary) and how she was tempted to fetch the book and actually read a passage aloud to him, to know what he thought, to clarify some doubt, to see if such-and-such theory could be applicable to India. She is working on the principle that to consult a man is to make him feel like a king, and to report to him is to make him feel like a god. She tells him that she was ironing his clothes. Or, that she scrubbed the toilet clean. She continues to enumerate her list with a note of requisite humility until a look of satisfaction flashes across his face.

He tells her something that happened during his day but his words are muted. The camera only sees, only shows, how attentively she listens. What he says can be anything really: how he came to the rescue of his department head, how he managed to solve a problem with the student body, how he discovered amazing talent in a young man, how he saved his colleague from making a blunder in her research hypothesis, how he presented *The Wretched of the Earth* in a mind-blowing fashion to his class. Whatever exploit is

19

recounted with gentle false-modesty she hangs on every word; she borders on rapture.

Soon, he settles in with his laptop, begins making phone calls to his friends. She fetches him a cup of coffee. She asks him what he wants to eat, and, in the meantime, fixes him a quick snack of *dosa* with peanut chutney. She goes to the kitchen, begins preparing an elaborate dinner. The scene fades out on a cutting board piling up with red slivers of chopped onion. In the background, we hear her hum a Tamil song, 'Yaaro, yaarodi, unnoda purushan?'

* *

And cut! I am the wife playing the role of an actress playing out the role of a dutiful wife watching my husband pretend to be the hero of the everyday. I play the role with flair.

The longer I stretch the act of the happily married couple, the more I dodge his anger. It's not a test of talent alone. My life depends upon it.

* *

It's not just the acting that I have to consider, though. I'm responsible for the whole, flattened film that has become my life. I think of camera angles. I think of how I should preserve the intricacies of the set. I must manage to capture what it means for a once-nomad to be confined to the four walls of a house. I must figure out a way to show on screen how even a small space of confinement begins to grow in the mind of the woman who inhabits it with her sorrows, how the walk from the bedroom to the door of the house becomes a Herculean task, or how the thought of checking on the slow-cooking chicken Chettinad curry when she is busy reading a book becomes an impossible chore. I also have to find out the technique to show its exact opposite, how the rooms begin to close in on this woman when she is being violated, how the walls chase her into corners, how the house appears to shrink the minute her husband is home, how there is nowhere to run, nowhere to hide, nowhere to evade his presence.

I am tone-deaf, but as the composer I need to consider mood-music. Church bells, the early morning on the move, the drop-dead stillness of afternoons, the chaos of every evening, the cawing of crows that mark the dying of the light, the slow way the grating noise of crickets seeps in to announce the night, broken only by the heavy trucks that take to the empty streets. This is how the world outside sneaks up to her, this is how she feels herself transported outside. I decide that among other domestic noises, the incessant patter of falling rain will be crucial to the soundtrack. This rainsong will have to be modulated to suit each scene where it is being used. Thunder rolling in the distance to accentuate marital tensions. The gradual showdown of a drizzle to signal the end of a moment of despair. Lightning, blue or pink or purple or blinding white, a sensory warning lighting up her sleeping figure before the rumbling skies jolt her awake. Electricity that plays truant, leaving the bickering couple drenched in darkness from one moment to the next. I contemplate the right response to every provocation, I cross out lines of dialogue when I realize that silence sinks in better. Here, I am the actress, the self-anointed director, the cinematographer and the screenplay writer. Every role that falls outside of being a wife affords me creative freedom. The story changes every day, every hour, every single time I sit and chart it out. The actors do not change, I cannot escape the set, but with every shift in my perspective, a different story is born. For a movie that will never be made and never hit the screen, I have already prepared the publicity material.

TWELVE ANGRY MEN (IN BED)

This movie shows a young, bohemian writer being recruited by her desperate husband to campaign in favour of a Communist Revolution. He unwittingly believes that sex involves more than body fluids, and convinced that he is injecting ideology into his crazy wife, he brings eleven angry men to bed each night, inadvertently jeopardizing his own position as the object of her desire.

Sometimes terrific, sometimes tedious, the company of Hegel, Marx, Engels, Lenin, Stalin,

Mao, Edward Said, Gramsci, Zizek, Fanon and
the quintessential Che Guevara proves to be a
bad influence. Quickly realizing that the more she
changes, the more things remain the same, the writer
begins to essay the mock role of an intellectual
in a bid to save her marriage. Faking orgasmic
delight in discussing the orthodoxy of the Second
International, or dismissing the postmodern idea of
deconstruction, she coasts along with aplomb. As a
spoof, combining pretentious intellectual orgies and
humdrum domesticity, this bawdy bedside romp
features twelve angry men and one bewitching writer
who is busy plotting her escape from their ideological
clutches.

Showcasing fearless acting and dialogue that is
simultaneously hilarious and horrifying, this comic
avalanche is guaranteed to be a crowd-pleaser.

III

Men are worthless, to trap them
Use the cheapest bait of all, but never
Love, which in a woman must mean tears
And a silence in the blood.

KAMALA DAS, 'A LOSING BATTLE'

Like a lot of writers, I thought of myself as someone belonging to the broad Left. I did not know where exactly this broad Left was, but I knew that I was there. I was the type who had bought a Che Guevara badge as a fifteen-year-old, and would have slept with him had I not been underage and had he not been long dead. I loved Bob Marley the same way. I had fallen in love with the rolling Rs of Spanish listening to Fidel Castro's 'History Will Absolve Me' speech. I belonged to that 1980s generation of Indian kids who were brought up on Soviet children's literature and magazines. Ants and astronauts and painted foxes and firebirds and sunbeam bunnies and humpbacked horses and little soldiers and magical creatures with flaming hair, all working for the common good and crusading against the evils of greed and selfishness. I knew these stories better than any of my own land. I loved Russia and her bitter cold that killed the Nazis, her Soviet snows that saved the world.

And then we watched it all melt away. My parents mourned for a week when the USSR fell, they called Gorbachev every murderous Tamil slur they could think of, until the news moved on and the Soviet dream moved into memory. But I didn't give up hope so easily. My blood still ran *red*.

I attended a youth camp about Cuba and watched a documentary on its young doctors. I filled two entire shelves with all the titles I could find in Chennai that were from Progress Publishers, Moscow. I read and even reread the Communist Manifesto. I lived in a dream that had long been left behind as dead. The dream had to be resurrected. Capitalism was ruining the world, there was no question about it. We needed an alternative way of living, a different way of organizing society. I was twenty-six, I thought I was doing all I could.

And then, in the course of running an online campaign against the death penalty, I met the man who was going to become my husband. I was enchanted. He was a college lecturer, but as far Left as they came and as orthodox as it was possible to be. He wore his outlaw air with charm, his Communist credentials without guile. He had been a Naxalite guerrilla ('Maoist', he corrected me). An underground revolutionary. He had assumed at least ten different names in less than three years. He spoke many languages, but he wouldn't tell me which, for fear of giving away too much information over the phone. He told me that I would learn all the little details in the course of our comradeship. The element of danger provided an irresistible aura around him. I loved this sense of adventure. I loved his idealism, I found the dogmatic obsession endearing. To fight the evils of capitalism, we required the staunchest warriors. He was one, and he could make one out of me.

In one of our earliest phone conversations he said we should be fighting LPG. I knew about Liquefied Petroleum Gas, the red, fourteen-kilo cylinders that were door-delivered twice every month and allowed us to cook at home. I agreed readily, and spoke of the need for organic bio-fuel. He did not seem impressed. Perhaps he assumed I was a hippy. It must have been the way I mentioned the word organic, dwelling inside each of its consonants, building myself a treehouse in one and a raft on another. I was wrong. *Do you not know that LPG stands for Liberalization-Privatization-Globalization? Really?*

To his credit, he was a man who gave me chances. Because of my stupid response in the first round, he asked me if I at least knew what MLM stood for. The man was fastidious with his acronyms, that much I could see. This time I cheated. I did not want my ignorance to come between him and me. I Googled. And I was convinced that Google was right because this seemed to be something to do with capitalist economics, and I replied, 'Multi-Level Marketing.' He laughed and, after what seemed like an interminable pause on the phone, said he wished he had the courage to cry instead.

MLM, or ma-le-ma, stood for Marxism-Leninism-Maoism, and it was the only politics that would liberate people. He sighed. I was too caught up in a middle-class lifestyle to know about issues that were affecting the people, he solemnly informed me. I had to leave all that behind if my

29

writing was going to be for the sake of the people's better-ment. I was willing to learn, I said.

* *

'Have you read *A Glass of Water and Loveless Kisses*?' he once asked me in a text. Was he trying to flirt with me? Why else would he drop a word like kiss in the middle of a serious Communist conversation?

'No. I haven't. Did you write it?'

A barrage of LMAOs, ROFLs.

'NO. No way. That's Lenin and Clara Zetkin.'

'Oh! But that's just Lenin on the Women's Question. It was his conversations with Zetkin, wasn't it? Of course I have read it. And had issues, comrade.'

'Oh. What did the feminist find there that offended her?'

'I think he had some unpleasant things to say about women when he talked about the sex-is-as-trivial-as-drinking-a-glass-of-water theory.'

'Such as?'

'Wait, let me pull out the exact quote for you. Here: "To be sure, thirst has to be quenched. But would a normal person normally lie down in the gutter and drink from a puddle? Or even from a glass whose edge has been greased by many lips?" Now, I find that very offensive. As a feminist, I would never look at myself as a gutter, or a glass greased by many lips.'

'Hmm. Interesting.'

'Is that all you have to say?'

'Well, Comrade Lenin offends you. I may not share your view, but I can recognize it. But when I read this book for the first time, I realized how much my actions were offending Lenin, his theory, and Communism itself. This book made me a better man, a better comrade.'

'How did *you* end up offending your Comrade Lenin?'

'There's a part where Lenin talks about how men, even so-called Marxists, take advantage of the idea of emancipation of love which is nothing but the emancipation of the flesh, to have one love affair after another. And Lenin condemns such promiscuity in sexual matters as nothing but bourgeois. And that made me feel guilty – feel guilty as to whether all my talk of emancipation and freedom with my women comrades had only been with the motive of making them fall in love with me. Was my talk of their sexual freedom only an excuse that would allow me to sleep with them? I realized the liberties I had taken with Communism. I felt like a cheat, an imposter.'

I was stunned and impressed. What he felt was not anger at Lenin, as I had, but anger at himself. He had a combination of introspection and honesty that burned with the violence of fire.

That conversation was the clincher.

This man is the real deal, I thought.

He was going to make me look at everything differently.

* *

Soon after my marriage I realized that my husband did not hate the Bill Gates and the Warren Buffetts and the Ambani Brothers of this world and the Indian state as much as he hated petit bourgeois writers (read, me). As a self-proclaimed 'true Maoist', he embarked upon a thorough class analysis of me and, based upon his disappointed findings, decided to set me on the right path. Marriage became a Re-education camp. He transformed into a teacher, and I became the wife-student learning from this Communist crusader.

Q: Where does the sun set?
A: On the ruling classes, who exploit the working masses.

Q: What does the sky hold?
A: The red star.

Q: And who holds up the sky?
A: Women hold up half the sky.

Q: What do we live for?
A: The Revolution.

Q: What is the Revolution?
A: The Revolution is not a dinner party. The Revolution is not writing an essay. The Revolution is not painting a picture. The Revolution is not doing

embroidery. A Revolution cannot be so refined, so leisurely and gentle, so temperate and kind and courteous and restrained and magnanimous. The Revolution is like tasting a pear. If you want to know what a pear tastes like, you must eat it yourself. If you want to know the theory and methods of Revolution, you must take part in Revolution because all genuine knowledge originates in direct experience.

Q: Where does one gain direct experience?
A: By learning from the masses and by teaching them.

Q: What is love?
A: ...

Q: I said, what is love?
A: Communism?
Q: Correct! And what is Communism?
A: Love?
A: No! Communism is not love; it is a hammer we use to correct ourselves and to crush our enemies.

So, in the end, it adds up to this: I must learn, and I must change. There is no other way. The scorching criticism that I once admiringly saw him deploy on himself had now found a new target. Throughout the period of instruction, my husband tells me that it's not sufficient to know the written word alone. That's what differentiates religions relying on the dogma of holy books and Communism. It is not only the Little Red Book that I must learn and imbibe. I must learn from the people around me. I must learn that walking to the grocery store without a *dupatta* on top of my tunic makes people frown because I am not respecting their standards of decency; I must learn that my husband does not hold my hand in public out of respect for the people's social mores; I must learn that a Communist only ever takes the bus because it is the transport of the people (unless he is late for a seminar he is giving and then he can take an auto-rickshaw); I must remember that the responsibility of the female body belongs to me, and that I must not move or walk in such a fashion that makes others feel it is an object of allurement and enjoyment (although I should respectfully tolerate the gropes, the whistles, the hissed invitations); I must learn that a Communist woman is treated equally and respectfully by comrades in public but can be slapped and called a whore behind closed doors. This is dialectics.

* *

Long before I signed up for Communism 101 (Marriage Course), I led a fairly normal, fairly eventless, fairly middle-class life, with very little drama – no starvation, no orphanage, no refugee crisis, no asylum-seeking, no incest, no jail term, no ISIS, no jihadi boyfriend, no Tamil Tiger

husband, no child marriage, no semi-successful suicide attempts, no precocious achievements, no parents undergoing
divorce or unemployment or affairs or bankruptcy. In the
middle of all that non-drama, what kept me occupied as a
teenager was the Quest for One True Love, the kind of love
that happened only in Tamil movies where the man is a hero
of the people, the underdog who takes down the bad guys,
the stammering-shy-orphan who cannot contain his anger
in the face of injustice, the undercover-cop-with-a-heart, the
misunderstood student-activist, the stylish go-getter who
never gives a fuck about what happens in the world until
someone threatens his girl. Try as hard as I might, however,
it was not going to be an easy task for a young woman like me
to find a young man like that.

Having said that, even for someone whose lack of good
looks had to be compensated and placated by vague compliments such as 'hot' and 'sultry' and 'smouldering' – all of
which are better suited to describe Chennai's weather than
one of its women – I left behind a long chain of broken hearts
and bruised egos and devdases and majnus and romeos and
salims and kattabommans and atthai payyans. Men offered
themselves up, eager garlanded goats, all ready for sacrifice.
They came to me with juvenile verse, with funny jokes, with
unlikely calculus doubts, with a month's used bus tickets I
had carelessly discarded and they had dutifully collected,
with a sheepish grin on their faces and a love letter hidden in

a textbook they had borrowed from me. They asked me for my phone number, dialled home and stayed silent when they heard my father on the other end. They added me on Yahoo Messenger and died their little deaths when they saw the small round user-status next to my screenname turn green and by the time they had plucked up the courage to type something, I was offline again, absent-mindedly pondering on the strange men from around the world who were flirting with me, who were confiding in me their deepest secrets, who trusted me because they believed that I was a 36D who wore red-lace panties.

Diplomacy helped me get rid of most male attention, but it did not help me in the Quest for One True Love. Not having found this man was a big curse in itself – I had handled male admiration rather ruthlessly, fending off suitors without offering the poor things even a chance to have a coffee together, let alone a foray into my underwear – and now I was left with the disadvantage of being a young woman of marriageable age with no history of romantic involvement, other than tangling myself in the bedsheets at 2 a.m. and getting lost in the quaint fantasy of being ravaged by Rhett Butler. I had never been kissed. I had never been Tamil-kissed even. So, by the time I finished college, I made up my mind that love does not come to those who stay nailed to one place reading Mills & Boon. I decided to move.

* *

Leaving home proved difficult. It would have been easier if I was a standard-issue engineer who was going to America for a master's degree. That would have allowed my father to boast each day to every colleague; it would have fulfilled my mother's reason for living, making her feel superior to her neighbours and thus providing the much sought-after meaning in life. They would have swelled with pride, perhaps dangerously so, endangering an artery here, popping out a varicose vein there. Instead, their only daughter was only going to Kerala, just a dodgy neighbouring state, doing one of those five-year integrated MA degrees that held no charm, required no intellectual prowess, and did not even further one's job prospects. 'Everyone from Kerala comes here to study, but our unique daughter decides to go there. What can I do?'

My father's intermittent grumbling was amplified by my mother who spoke non-stop about sex-rackets, ganja, alcoholism and foreign tourists, making Kerala – a demure land of lagoons and forty rivers – appear more and more like Goa. Realizing that I wasn't easily scared, she even attempted to incite jealousy telling me of the legendary allure of Malayalee women, and expected me to drop my plan in a last minute fit of insecurity. As much as her revelation irked me, I found the perfect retort: 'I am going there to s-t-u-d-y, Mom, not for a beauty contest.' She pretended not to hear me.

With their concerted campaign against Kerala having failed, they were sophisticated enough to switch to a new plan of attack. Mom wept for days on end, Dad wept because she was weeping. They took turns to come to my room, sit on a chair, and cry. My mom confessed that she did not want to face her husband alone every day and begged me not to leave. Dad claimed that without my calming presence in the house, he would never have a peaceful evening because my mom was hell-bent on sending him to an early grave with endless fights.

They anticipated that their marriage would unravel without me; they foresaw a future where they would waste away alone and there would be no daughter at their death-bed; they blamed television, newspapers, radio stations and my best friend for putting such a funny idea into my head; and when everything else failed, they blamed me roundly squarely quadrilaterally for being ungrateful and thoughtless and selfish, and at the end of many weeks of failed emotional blackmail, they had to give in, and make peace with the fact that I was indeed moving out.

* *

I rapidly settled into university life. I studied language and literature by day and I found the nerve to let my hair down at night. I treated men like an equal opportunities employer. I flirted. I forged friendships.

The men I liked here quoted Neruda. They read Márquez

in the Malayalam. A train running late, a hartal on exam day, an inability to get movie tickets, the unending queues in the beverage store – all of that, they termed Kafkaesque. They spoke of Theodorarkis and Kakogiannis and asked me to watch *Zorba the Greek* with them. They wrote poems. They peppered their conversations with popular film dialogues, to which I lacked all frames of reference. At the first sign of monsoon clouds, they sang Rafi – '*aaj mausam bada beimaan hai*' – hand-picked to attribute their attempts at seduction to the weather, to the state of the skies, to the smell of eager, just-drenched earth. They mimicked Rajinikanth, and when they became intimate enough, they broke into Tamil songs to please me. They were veterans of the heartbreak, they carried the war-wounds of love in their beards. They rocked their *mundus*, wore them just about everywhere. They drank rum and whisky and brandy, and, out of loyalty to Russia, they made their toasts with vodka. They attempted clumsy passes, asked for hugs with the persistence of two-year-olds asking for candy, apologized the next morning on behalf of the alcohol that made them overstep their boundaries, and did the exact same thing the next time. And one fine day, totally out of the blue, they swore to kill themselves because I was not reciprocating their feelings.

I soaked up all that drama.

* *

There was Anish, who never met me outside of college, who was content with gazing into my eyes and scribbling my name on his notebooks, he of the respectable-love that did not breach boundaries, the love that fertilized in place of fucking insanely, the love where a woman was treated (almost) like a sister until the day of her marriage, the love of a shy and uncertain man-boy, with a moustache still growing in patches, with a love that started as a failed mission, a love that moved on.

Balakrishnan, who saw in me the earthiness of Ilayaraja's music, and in me he claimed to uncover the wide-eyed, strong-willed, quick-to-retort, dancing-in-the-rain *Mouna Raagam* Revathi, the kind of woman the men of my father's generation fantasized about, the woman whose touch was electric, whose speech was sharp as sickles, who coupled old-world shrewdness with rustic naïveté, and the longer he kept projecting this image on me, the more distant I grew from myself, and from him.

Chandran, thin and tall and dark and bearded, who took me to his rehearsals, who I met when I auditioned for a play, who was adapting *The Last Temptation of Christ* for the stage, whose life revolved around theatre, but for whom drama was insufficient, for whom being in love meant being alive, and that meant not holding to an emotion long enough for it to gather moss, but instead changing, changing, changing it all the time, through fate and force and fuck-ups just so that every moment of his life his heart was bleeding on a jagged edge, and he could feel and feel and feel.

Dinesh, a friend of Azhar's, who came to me to ask if the text on his start-up website had any grammatical errors, who talked and talked and talked with me, all of it centred around him, but even in the midst of the chatter, I had the opportunity to discover that he was an excellent kisser, and I would have allowed my days to whirl into his tongue, but the kilometres of his speech was not the road I wanted to take, and so I left him, not out of dislike, not out of malice, but because I was looking for respite from unceasing conversation.

Edwin, the little rich boy, the boy who was exploring himself, who was into jazz and marijuana one week, poetry and Faiz and Pound by the weekend, the wannabe painter who wrote songs for me, the impresario who wanted me to appreciate Monet and Cézanne, who begged me to read Susan Sontag, who took me to hidden-away beaches to photograph me because he was madly in love with my imperfections, but I could not cope with his erratic pursuit of art and beauty, and I was filled with the sudden dread that the world so painstakingly built around him could be shattered any second, and so I moved away from him, a star spiralling out of axis to save a little of its own light.

Faizal, who briefly flitted into my life, who carried clouds of depression on his small, stooped shoulders, who spoke of shadows whispering in his head, who spoke of shadows stitched to his feet, who dismissed my words of love as dew-drops on dead, decaying leaves, who lived in a drunken stupor until the ginger-skinned moon appeared in the sky, and then he would make his way to me, and hold me close, and breathe my rain-tree smell to feel safe, and his night would come to an end in my arms, until one day the demons in his head took hold of him, and he became caught up in his little world of sadness, and I was afraid to enter, and he was afraid to walk out and we left it there, in some place where words could not reach.

Girish, a college lecturer, whose radar was quick to sense my restlessness, who was even quicker to offer a hand of friendship, who revealed to me after a week of acquaintance that his wife never consummated their marriage, and try as hard as he could to elicit a sympathy fuck from me, it went nowhere, it only soured our friendship, and so he told the entire college that I tried to seduce him, and almost everyone seemed to buy his story, except the women who had been similarly solicited, who saw him for what he was.

A is B is C is D is E is F is G is H is I

And J is K is L is M is N is O is P is Q

And R is T is V is W is some X-Y-Z.

Not all their stories need to be written down here.

Sunil could have been Sudheer could have been Satish could have been Surya could have been Sareesh could have been Sunny could have been Sandeep.

The names of the men do not matter. It can be switched any which way on the page, and my story will remain the same. They were all strangers, they all became friends of some sort, and as much as they furthered my limited knowledge of what it meant to be the object of a man's affection, I lost my heart to none of them. I fooled around, hoping that eventually, perhaps, some love would appear. Some boundaries were breached. Some boundaries were redefined. Some boundaries became borders with a vigilant army camping along their length. I lost some, I learnt some.

* *

For all the arbitrariness of my pursuit, the absence of maps and the lack of light from fading fast-dying stars, I one day steered my restless paper-boat heart towards a safe anchor.

He came from the coast, a creature of the sea. His words were rough winds and stormy waters – but, in all that agitation, I found the man I had always longed for. My One True Love. I was swept away, falling for him before realizing he was a famous politician and before realizing it was doomed before we had even shared our first kiss.

Let me tell you a dream. Far away from seascapes, deep in the forest ranges of central Kerala, I encounter a leopard. I am transfixed by his eyes. Being the catwoman that I am, I stroke him on the head, I scratch him at the scruff of his neck, I let him sniff me. He plays with me. He even lets me rub his belly.

MEENA KANDASAMY

Then, suddenly, in the blink of an eye, his feline teeth find my flesh, my hand is mauled, my heart is left bleeding. That is how the dream ends. The reality intercedes later.

This One True Love – which flourished for two, three years – left me wounded. I spent months scooped in bed howling my heart out. In learning to forget him, I had to pick up what was left of me, the little fragments of individuality, scattered across the scenery of our love, like broken bangles, chipped glass, colourful pebbles. Trinkets of the type crows love to gift, and small children love to collect.

This was a lover who had become the landscape. Everything in Kerala reminded me of him. The never-ending sea made me feel abandoned. Lonely riverbanks made me weep inconsolably. Dawn breaking, over pink-and-cement skies, drove me into despair. Political graffiti anguished me. The city became his ruthless messenger. I had to renounce this life and return home to my parents.

Back in the boredom of Chennai, and to escape the frowns of my parents, I grabbed every freelance job I could get, I volunteered my time to online activism, I filled up my calendar hoping that being busy would help me cope with heartbreak. At this vulnerable moment I met the man I would marry.

There was no dull ache of desire in this manhunt. I was only looking for safety. In turn, he appeared to carry two inbuilt safeguards: unlike the politician, as a college lecturer, he was perfect husband-material in the eyes of my parents. Unlike

WHEN I HIT YOU

the politician, in his secret life as a guerrilla, he believed in a revolutionary overthrow of the Indian state, boycotted democratic structures, and I could be sure of the absence of electoral ambitions that would thwart a life together.

I rushed into it.

The rest, as they say, is the unrest of this story.

IV

In using there are always two.
The manipulator dances with a partner who cons herself.
There are lies that glow so brightly we consent
to give a finger and then an arm
to let them burn.
I was dazzled by the crowd where everyone called
    my name.
Now I stand outside the funhouse exit, down the slide
reading my guidebook of Marx in Esperanto
and if I don't know anymore which way means forward
down is where my head is, next to my feet
with a pocketful of words and plastic tokens.

MARGE PIERCY, 'SONG OF THE FUCKED DUCK'

Remember the *Ramayana* post-reunion story.

Suspicious King Husband tells Rescued Queen Wife to walk through fire – if she was chaste through their period of separation, she'll emerge untouched, else, she will be consigned to ashes. All or Zilch. She comes out clean as Evian, but immediately commands Mother Earth to swallow her, outraged by her man's suspicious behaviour. She was First Lady in Valmiki's epic, and in keeping with the social practices of the times, this kind of test was a public spectacle.

Not so for me. Not so at Primrose Villa.

Not with a Communist husband. Fuck monarchy. Fuck the feudalism of petty warlords. Here, he burns himself, causing no harm whatsoever to the damsel-in-distress. Here, the test takes place before the opportunity to cheat arises, as a pre-emptive, preventive measure.

We are in the kitchen, having coffee.

He lights a match, brings it to his bare left elbow, extinguishes it against his skin. I smile nervously. Then another match is lit.

'What kind of party trick is that?' I ask.

'Are you listening?'

'Yes.'

Another lit match. Another self-inflicted ordeal.

I do not get the joke.

'So, I have your attention.'

His head tilted to the right. He is staring at me intensely.

'Yes, sir' – I'm tempted to say, but I don't.

'Yes. Of course I'm listening. You don't have to burn your-self, for god's sake.'

'Come off Facebook.'

'What?'

'*Come off Facebook.*'

'I heard you the first time. But why the hell?'

'I'm going to keep doing this until you see my point.'

'Darling, please cool down. What's your point? What have you got against Facebook?'

'There is no reason why you should be on Facebook. It's narcissism. It's exhibitionism. It's a waste of time. I've said this to you a thousand times. It's merely you voluntarily feeding information straight to the CIA, to the RAW, to the IB, to everyone who is hounding my life. Every fucking thing is being monitored. Your life may be a peep show, but I'm a revolutionary. I cannot let you endanger me. We've had this argument so often that I've lost count. I'm not going to repeat everything I've said.'

I could smell the match heads and the burnt hair.

'This is plain and simple blackmail. I'm not going to do anything if you blackmail me.'

WHEN I HIT YOU

'I don't have to tell you what to do. You're pushing me into this corner where I'm forced to tell you what's good for you and what is not.'

'If you put the matches down, we can talk about Facebook.'

'If you love me, this is the quickest way you will make up your mind.'

For a split second, I think about taking a matchstick and burning my own skin. His aim is to make me suffer for his pain; I do not want to suffer two-fold by inflicting this bizarre punishment on myself. Another matchstick is lit and put out. And another and another. I've stopped counting. It almost makes me feel that he is enjoying himself.

As distressed as I am, there's a part of me wanting to laugh. This elaborate ruse of revolution being roped in. This standard, textbook mention of the CIA and the home-grown RAW to frighten me. To laugh at my husband would mean that I humiliate him, the consequences of which would be far worse than the matchstick pyrotechnical performance. To reason with him will lead to a long, interminable fight, a war of attrition that would exhaust me into defeat.

I look at him, deciding what I should do next. Now the lit matches are being extinguished on the inside of his left forearm, each leaving a tiny red welt on the skin. He doesn't look up at me, he doesn't say a word, and that in itself scares me. He has the defiant eyes of a man who is in no mood to give up. I do not know where this will end.

In the next ten minutes, I deactivate my Facebook account.

It is my lifeline to the world outside. Since moving to Mangalore, Facebook has transformed into my only remaining professional link. Here, I do not have the circle of artist friends I had in Kerala, I do not have the family networks that I had in Chennai. In this isolation, Facebook helps me promote my work, gives me news, keeps me in the loop of the literary scene, allows me to have an online presence which is pivotal if I do not want to be forgotten in a freelance world. My husband is not unaware of this. He knows that my being a writer involves being at the mercy of others, being visible, being remembered at the right time so that someone throws an opportunity my way. In my precarious situation, when he wants me to cut myself off from Facebook, I know that it is an act of career suicide. Right now, arguing with him will not get me anywhere. I simply count myself lucky that he asks me only to 'deactivate' and not actually delete my Facebook account.

To save face, and to explain the sudden departure, I put up my last status message, telling the world that I'm busy with a writing project, that I need time for myself, that this is going to be a long hiatus.

* *

When I was offering myself out as a freelancer in Chennai, having escaped Kerala and heartbreak – and in order to escape the boredom of being back in my parents' place – I did some ghost-translation for an old man in the neighbourhood, sub-contracting for the *UNESCO Courier*. I was asked to render into Tamil a rather long essay about the human endeavour to communicate with aliens.

Of all the things we could have said to the people of other planets, we chose to fire into space a capsule containing the model for the double helix structure, the composition of DNA and the formula of its nucleotides. Not a message that declared: *it is sunny here it also rains a lot we love colours and dope we sing and we dance we cook up a storm with anything we can find we are fucked up in too many ways but we are a funny bunch so may we request the pleasure of your company.*

For a message that would take twenty-five thousand years to send, and another twenty-five thousand years to receive a reply, we had no sense of humility or hospitality. We were clearly showing off.

My communication with the world outside falls into this pattern. When I am forced to leave Facebook, my final message is not: *Trouble in Second Week of Marriage: Husband-Moron Insistent I Stay Isolated. Mr Control Freak Blackmailed Me Into Deactivating Account. Writer At Risk! SOS!*

Instead, my swansong is serious and formal; I write about the intertwining double helix of projects and looming dead-lines. I compose the picture of being a busy woman, and maintain the act to its precise proportions. I write out the formulaic pretence of living the writer's life. No one gets a clue of how precariously alone I feel.

* *

My abrupt disappearance from Facebook is the first of several stages. The same week, he writes down his email password and gives it to me.

'You can have this.'

'I do not need it.'

'I trust you.'

'Okay.'

'Do you trust me?'

'I do. So?'

'Do you trust me enough to share your passwords?'

'I have never shared my passwords with anyone.'

'So, you are hiding something?'

'No.'

'How would I know?'

'By believing me.'

'How would I believe you if you don't trust me?'

'Because I have nothing to hide.'

This argument is endless, it keeps moving in circles, a snake eating its own tail. At the moment, the only way of proving myself means writing down all my passwords. My hot tears burn my cheeks, but I resolutely buy myself an uneasy peace. I write down my passwords.

The camel's nose has just entered the tent.

* *

Unlike the Arab and his camel, we are married to each other. A month into the marriage, I find that he has answered some of my emails.

'I can handle my own messages, I never asked you to do this.'

He does not defend himself. He does not argue. He whistles a tune, continues to fiddle with his computer.

'Come here, my little one, come here,' he says. The taunt in his voice is like the slime in a deep, old well – glinting, slippery, deathly.

He opens his own inbox and shows me that he has been replying to his emails by signing both our names at the end of every message. I find that my name has been co-signed in letters to students, in group emails to his activist friends, in making book recommendations to his colleagues, in querying for a postcolonial studies research conference, for all sundry little shit. I feel nauseous. I feel robbed of my identity. I'm no longer myself if another person can so easily claim to be me, pretend to be me, and assume my life while we live under the same roof.

I gather myself enough to ask: 'How long has this been going on?'

'Since we got married.' His voice is flat now. Matter-of-fact.

Precise and reasonable like a well-paved six-lane highway.

And then, unfazed, he tries to elaborate: 'I want the world to know that we are a couple. I want them to accept us as a unit.'

* *

My mother on the phone:
Listen, my dear. I know it is upsetting. Just breathe deeply. Do not give him any ground for suspicion. Let us see how far he goes. Suspicion is in the nature of men; it is in the nature of love. He revolves around one question: What if she loves somebody else?

It is a weak mind, it is a weak man who comes up with these fears. Do not let him feel weak. If he wants your world to revolve around him, make that happen. He will grow tired of your attention, and he will learn to give you space. The more you try to stake your claim to privacy, the more he will assume that you are hiding things from him and forging a secret life for yourself. That will drive him mad. Stay open, and that dog will leave you in peace when he cannot catch scent of all the shit that he thinks exists.

* *

It begins to fit a pattern.

The first to go was my phone.

When I had just moved with him to Mangalore after

the marriage, it wouldn't cease ringing for hours – friends, well-wishers, distant family – calling me up to congratulate the happy couple, asking for details, chiding me on why it was all so hush-hush and hasty. Roaming charges, Tamil curiosity and all their warm cheer made me run out of credit by the end of the evening. We kept topping it up for a day and the next, and then my comrade-husband advised me on the economics of it all, the exorbitant costs I would be paying if I retained the number of another state, and suggested that it was better if I got a local number. The task of procuring the new number was taken on as his own personal responsibility – we could have walked over to any little shop, given a photocopy of his ID card to prove our address and a passport-sized photo and got a SIM card for fifty rupees, but it was not so easy where he was concerned. He was paranoid about the state, about security, about being monitored. He deemed it best if the SIM card was procured in the name of one of his students' extended friendship circle, someone whose connections to him would not be apparent, someone who would not be on the police radar.

That promised card materialized after ten days of religious waiting, and when it finally reached me, my husband instructed me not to share the number indiscriminately, warning me that the moment a friend of mine in the press or media or publishing industry got hold of the number, it was the equivalent of uploading it online for all to see.

'There's a reward on my head. Two lakhs, last heard. They are this close, my dear, this fucking close to finding me. What shields me? They do not know that the so-called underground, dangerous, armed guerrilla they are looking for is a happily married college lecturer now. Don't play with fire. You will be throwing us in jail. Torture. A staged "encounter". The police will take me from home for an interrogation, then come back to speak with you. They will be polite as hell, they will even drink the tea you make for them, and two days later, you will read in the papers that a most-wanted, armed thirty-year-old man in combat fatigues was shot dead by the paramilitary in some far-away forest. The same polite policemen will turn up at our house again and ask you to come and identify my body. You will become a widow overnight. Do you want any of that? Am I making it clear?'

I nod in agreement. This is something I had never anticipated. I want to tell him that I will never, ever betray him, but I do not know if that is something he wants to hear. Apart from my parents, I do not share my phone number with anyone else. Even to my parents, I do not breathe a word about his paranoia – about his fear of being captured for waging war against the state, or the risky side of the man I have married, and how all this in effect restrains me. Tomorrow, if trouble were to knock on our door, I do not want anyone else to pay a price.

* *

The loss of telephonic communication doesn't wound me too much. But what I find impossible to fathom is how I now find myself in the position of having my online freedom curtailed. I never thought that it would be so important to me until it was.

His voice drowns out all my arguments with one sentence: *You are addicted. You are addicted. You are addicted. You are addicted.*

In an act of mercy, he allows me three hours a week: rationed, it comes to a very brief half an hour a day. The internet access itself is possible only in his presence, for he carries the Huawei USB dongle with him at all times – saying he needs the internet to prepare for his classes and to do his research. I relay this problem to my parents, hoping that they can see through the absolute insanity of this prohibition. Mom, this is so fucked up. Dad, this is so fucked up. Mom and Dad, this will kill me as a writer. Mom and Dad, I will go mad. They do not get it.

Three hours is a long time, my mother replies, three hours a week will do. I only take ten minutes every day to check my email, she says.

Some days my students check email for me, she adds.

My father does not even have an email address. That does not prevent him from having an opinion. He believes the entire world of the internet is a big sinkhole waiting to swallow his daughter forever.

We brought you up without the TV, and you have turned out just fine, he says. Will you die if you do not have the internet? he asks me.

I answer in the affirmative.

The internet is your drug, he says.

Your husband is doing this for your own good, they both concur.

'Your own good' was the mantra of my mother when I was growing up – it justified being force-fed laxatives once every three months, not celebrating my birthdays at school, curfews against travelling alone, refusal of permission to go to picnics. 'Your own good' was the reason my English teacher offered when she pulled me by the ear and led me out of the classroom, shouting *rowdy girl rowdy girl rowdy girl this is for your own good* and struck me with a wooden ruler. 'Your own good' was what justified my teenage neighbour putting his fingers inside my eight-year-old vagina to check for forest insects and bed bugs and evil imps. When I hear 'your own good' I am reduced to being a child again. I do not argue any more. I go silent.

* *

Walk out. Walk out.

The recurrent voice that stays stuck in your throat. It is how you know you need to run. It is how you know that now is not the right time. How you also know there will never be a right time. How you know it is not the how of it that matters, but the when. How you know the world will laugh at you for a month-long marriage. Even that is not as cruel as the sight of the sad faces of your parents. Disgraced. You have given them nothing but disappointment. The defeat they will carry in their eyes for the rest of their days. Never again the old pride. Never again the easy trust. Never again will the way they say your name be the same. No more will they carry their dreams on your shoulders.

Not just them and their heavy, gathered sorrows. You will have to live with one person all your life: you. The you wanting to leave today might be the you who thinks you should have stayed tomorrow. The fear that when you face yourself ten years from now, you will blame your haste, blame your hot blood, blame your sharp tongue, blame yourself for giving up so easily. The question within you, coming from your own sense of fairness: what if he was given the chance to rectify his mistakes, to change himself, to begin anew? The next question, coming up after the commercial break: were you willing to forgive him? And then of course, the inevitable, the unavoidable, absolutely vital: have you fought enough for what you believe in?

Fight or Flight.

The old formula again. I haven't given up fighting, not yet.

The flight only comes when the fight has failed.

V

Sometimes, of course, art creates the
suffering in the first place.

ELFRIEDE JELINEK, *THE PIANO TEACHER*

What prevents a woman from walking out of an abusive relationship?

Old-school feminists will speak about economic independence. A woman is free if she has the money to support herself. With a job, she will find her feet. If she has a job, it will miraculously solve all her problems. A job will give her community. One day she will walk into the office, and they will ask her about the bruise above her eyebrow and she will say she walked into a wall, but they will know it is her husband hitting her, and they will wrap her up in a protective embrace. In the framework of a job, a woman will find that one female friend who will see her through thick and thin. The job will create a support group for her, people who will give her access to the police, to the lawyers, to the judges.

In the office, there will at least be one man – one good, honest, decent man – who finds her attractive, who slips her love notes at weekly meetings, who loves her for what she is, who makes her feel beautiful, who makes her laugh. In the absence of such a man, she will find a lesbian lover. Sometimes, the lesbian love happens irrespective of the presence or absence of men, the woman turning her back on an entire gender to live happily – and safely – ever after.

Abstractions are easy, but my story, like every woman's story, is something else.

* *

No one knows the peculiar realities of my situation.

How do you land a job when:

- you end up somewhere in the middle of the teaching semester?
- you have no contacts in a strange city?
- your husband has forced you off social media?
- you have no phone of your own?
- your husband monitors and replies to all messages addressed to you?
- you do not speak the local language?
- you have the wifely responsibility of producing children first?

That's a long list already. These are not the regrets of an un-employed person. These are the complaints of an imprisoned wife.

* *

Let's say that I'm even allowed to take a job. Will the daily escape from the house granted by a 9-to-5 solve my problem? Or, will that freedom act as a compensation for the deal with the devil that I seem to have made within my marriage? Will I breathe freely for a few hours and be happy to come home to this state of hate that awaits me? Will I get used to it, the new normal? Or, will this outside world step in and intervene? I do not have answers. In my short life as a wife so far in this town, I have participated in the same little verbal dance that happens every time I step out of the house and run into the neighbours, or on the rare day when I visit my husband in his college to hand him his lunch and I come across his students and friends.

How are you?

Have you eaten?

Do you like Mangalore?

Do you like the weather?

Do you like the rain?

Do you like the Mangalore food?

How was last weekend?

What's your plan this weekend?

Conversations here follow the same pattern. An endless back-and-forth relay of absolute pointlessness. No question demands an honest answer. A question is asked as an exercise in formal behaviour.

Questions that are greetings. Questions that are place-holders. Questions that fill awkward gaps. Questions to suggest an interest that does not exist. Questions that pretend to listen.

Never, ever a question that seeks to know.

It's a register, the kind of talk that's reserved for the new-wife-in-town, the talk that's meant for a stranger you've just met; in this cooperative talk, there is no point at which I can tell the truth.

* *

This was one of those things they taught us back in college. I marvelled at this feature of social interaction – surprised that it had a proper name, the 'Politeness Phenomenon' – and considered it a great achievement of our civilization. I believed we had reached the zenith of sophistication as we did this nervous foxtrot with strangers, never hurting, never making them reveal hurt. It had all been perfectly rehearsed and choreographed.

Two sociolinguists, Penelope Brown and Stephen Levinson, about whom I have no reliable gossip except that they are married to each other, put forth this theory. Their conjecture: people use politeness as a way of mutually permitted deception in order to help each other save face. Translation: in real life, unlike in an exam, no stranger will ask you a question that you will have trouble answering.

We were made to study this because it was a language universal, something that happened in every language across the world. At that time, it was reassuring.

Whatever its benefits for the rest of humankind, I have now come to look at it as a design flaw in the construct of language.

There's nothing in the structure of language to flash a code-red in the middle of polite verbal back-and-forth, nothing that can interrupt the staged niceness by being a secret cry for help.

* *

Trying to recollect the first time I was hit by my husband, there's only hot glass tears and the enduring fear of how often it has come to pass. The reconstruction of the events does not help. It always begins with a silly accusation, my denial, an argument, and along the road, the verbal clash cascades into a torrent of blows. The accusations stand out because of how trivial they are – Why does this man call you 'dearest'? Why have you cleared your trash can in your email inbox? Why are there only nine telephone calls on the call log of your phone, whose number have you deleted? Why haven't you washed the sink? Why are you trying to kill me by trying to over-salt my food? Why can't you write as 'anonymous'? Why did you not immediately reject the conference invitation when you bloody know that I'm not going to let you travel alone? – sometimes, his bones of contention are so thin that they make me wonder if any accusation is only a ruse and excuse to hit me.

I do not have anyone I can talk to about what is going on behind these closed doors. At the moment, I am not even sure if I want to talk to anyone about what I am going through.

On a dull afternoon, I can catalogue the weapons of abuse

that have gathered around the house. The cord of my Mac-Book which left thin, red welts on my arms. The back of the broomstick that pounded me across the length of my back. The writing pad whose edges found my knuckles. His brown leather belt. Broken ceramic plates after a brief journey as flying saucers. The drain hose of the washing machine.

I did not know that this was the exemplary life awaiting a newly married woman.

* *

Before we were married, we had discussed our plans. Rosy hazy red. Nothing was well defined; I liked it that way. Undecided, unprepared, spontaneous. All that I knew was that we would move to Mangalore, where he had a job lecturing in English Literature. I would take up a teaching assignment, hopefully at his college. Until that happened, I would try to write. Later, we would consider whether or not we liked the place and whether or not we would think of moving. We would be aimless. We would be unchained. We would stay afloat, anchored only to each other. We were making a leap into the wild. Hand in hand, ready to fall or float. To make it more exciting, we had blindfolds on. Or at least, I had a blindfold on.

That seems like a long, long time ago.

* *

'Why don't you come and teach my class one day? I can arrange it. You can occupy yourself.'

This comes as a gesture of reciprocal affection, a statement of appreciation for my efforts.

We have settled in properly: the fridge holds milk and eggs and *idli* batter; the ceiling fan's intermittent flapping noise no longer wakes us up at night; the cockroach situation in the kitchen is under control. The daily grind has been worn into place.

His offer comes after a campaign of very gentle nagging, to ask him if there are any opportunities for me.

Can I teach here? Can you ask around for me? Do you need a copy of my CV? Will I find something temporary? Don't you think it would be nice if I got out of the house once in a while?

'St Alfonso's does not allow married couples to work in the same institution, there is an employee policy against that,' he casually informs me one night when I am pressing him on progress. 'The sister college is a possibility, but the problem is that you have to wait until the next semester to try to get a job there.' This suggestion, that I can give a guest lecture to his students, is the big concession. Even his departmental head is happy with this arrangement.

A week later, just for an hour, I handle his class.

In the middle of my lecture on Postcolonial Literature, I spot a student passing a handwritten note. I ignore it, I carry on, but as the note travels, I'm forced to act. I approach their desks and take the piece of paper. *Please let all of us donate 50p each, and buy coconut oil and a comb for sir's wife. The loose hair looks like a beggar's.*

My cheeks burn, but I crumple the note into my palm and finish the class with as much dignity as I can muster. This is not my idea of a dream job, to stand before a room of fifty men and women who are judging my looks as I try to teach.

That afternoon, I tell this to my husband, the note still balled up in my pocket. He launches into a lecture on how often he has asked me to learn from the people; dress and behave in a way that they will respect. My first day out back-fires on me.

* *

Two days later, I have thought enough about the incident to formulate a fitting comeback to the student. Two days later, unfortunately, is a time-frame in which I've been reduced to irrelevance. The class that I was handling – on postcolonial-ism – was not entirely disconnected to the way in which I was being read. Hair is a vexed topic in the many subcultures that make up India: in the *Kamasutra*, a woman standing in the courtyard of her home, combing her untied hair, has been seen as the symbol of a wanton woman; the wild, untame-able hair of possessed women has been seen as the sign of the devil itself; the matted hair of women saints and the shorn head of widows, a symbol of their having given up all claims to exercising sexuality. Not a pretty picture by any means. Where and how does the monster of colonialism enter this picture and pose for a photograph?

The superficial backstory is not very hard to spot: shorter, untied, loose hair was seen as an influence of European women – a corruption of the local ideal; a symbolism of unbridled, shameless desires; an effort at modernity at the expense of tradition; a betrayal of the national through an allegiance to the white man through a replication of the white woman's styling. There's another apocryphal story that often lies buried. Regiments of the British Army had their retinue of native sex workers who stayed close to the cantonments. Unlike Nautch girls and *devadasis*, each of these sex workers was registered by the colonial government. In exchange for lodgings and a substantial soldier clientele, they had to agree to regular examination for venereal diseases. This was in the heyday when syphilis maimed more men than brutal Indian summers, so these women were forbidden from sleeping with the natives, out of misplaced fears.

The story goes that the dark, long tresses of these women would be chopped periodically – allowing the enforcers and sanitary inspectors to easily spot them at the marketplace if they were ever soliciting native men, and to drag them back to the Regiment. As much as it enabled control for the cause of the empire, in the eyes of the lay people, a woman with

short, loose hair in the bazaar also became synonymous with
the white man's prostitute. She was the one who was sleeping with the enemy, sexually servicing the oppressor, and she
deserved the greatest disdain.

In the six decades since the British left, some perceptions
do not seem to have changed. In our postcolonialism classes,
we speak of the empire writing back. But within these class-
rooms, we are still products of the same empire – carrying
our bags of shame and sin.

* *

When I try to unload my interpretation of the classroom
debacle to my husband, he is dismissive.

He begins thumping the table and laughing out loud.
'Finally you found an excuse. And what's that excuse?
Colonialism? You write in English – and you find it convenient enough to blame my students' opinion of you on
colonialism. Don't bullshit me. You know what? The whore
in those times was the link, the bridge between the colonizer
and the colonized. Today, the link – the writer who writes in
English, this bridge – she is the whore.'

* *

Being a writer invites constant ridicule from my husband.
At the end of a long day, he comes home to ask me what I
did all day long. I was writing, I say. More often, I stick to

the more modest version: I was trying to write. In the brief pauses between household chores, I would hunt for inspiration on empty pages, on the blank screen of my laptop. That's not work in his dictionary. That is someone doing nothing.

There is a semblance of respect that comes my way when I'm asked to write for a magazine, however. Even if the magazine itself is called into question by my husband, he recognizes that this validation might mean that he should take me more seriously. Usually, however, he decides against it.

Such as when *Outlook* wants an essay for their annual issue on sex surveys, and the editor emails me asking me to call so that I can be briefed. My husband and I are busy packing to catch a train that will take us to his village for a weekend with his family, but I manage to slip out and make the call.

When I share the details with my husband he says I have been asked to write on sexuality because I have the wide-ranging experience of having fucked men who are twenty years old, thirty years old, forty years old, fifty years old, sixty years old, seventy years old.

He is laughing but only to try to disguise his anger.

This is an accusation that I cannot share with anyone. The shaming that I face as I try to write this article is something my readers will never know about.

'Why did you agree,' he asks? 'You are a slave of this corporate media. You are selling your body. This is elite prostitution, where men do not get to touch you, but they masturbate to the image of the woman you represent. This is not freedom. This is sexual anarchy. This is not revolutionary. This is pandering to vulgar imperialist culture.'

And within the next hour, there are suggestions that I have slept with the entire editorial team at *Outlook*. The most intimate that I have been with any of them is that solitary phone call.

* *

'How do you propose to even write your sex article?' At the last minute, he takes my laptop out of my travel bag and leaves it on the table.

'This is going to stay here,' he says. 'Only the two of us are going on this trip. We are going to my village, to meet relatives, to attend a marriage, to stay with my mother. I do not want you to sit there and keep typing your essay when there are more important things to do. *Should I remind Writer Madam that she is also a wife?*'

There are no computers in the village. There is no internet either, and in any case, I cannot go to a net café in the nearest town without him by my side, or without his approval.

I snatch every free second I can get over the next two days. I type while I catch water to fill the pots in the house, when I enter the bathroom to wash my hair, when I'm asked to clean the moringa leaves for a soup, when I watch the goat stew simmer over a firewood stove and the smoke sets me coughing, when I babysit my niece and nephew. I learn to compose whole sentences and paragraphs at a stretch in my mind. It is an article that I entirely key in on my phone, a clunky Nokia E63. The new Mangalore SIM card that my husband has got for me does not have a data plan, and there is no way I can transmit my article. At some point, I want to call the editor at *Outlook* and read out what I have written for someone on his team to take down. The fear of being discovered midway through the call makes me hesitate. I search desperately for the right opportunity. Maybe when my husband goes off with one of his cousins on some errand, to pick up a surly guest, or to troubleshoot some last minute misunderstanding that has cropped up with the caterers – one of a thousand things that could go wrong at a wedding and would need a man's authority to interfere. All that I need is half an hour of freedom and I keep looking for the minute such a chance opens up.

My fear of him gives way to my fear of missing the deadline. In desperation, I come up with the riskiest of strategies. I remember that my husband and the USB dongle that allows us to connect to the internet are never parted. What makes the dongle an internet-ready device is the data-powered SIM card inside it. When he has gone off to have his evening bath, I rummage through the pockets of his clothes and find the dongle. I quickly remove the SIM card, hide it in the side seams of my *kurta*, and leave everything looking as untouched as before. When my turn to use the bathroom comes, I hurry inside, my phone well hidden within a towel, replace the SIM card, and send the article across a very slow Opera browser, with no formatting, no italics. When I bathe that night, looking at the black starlit sky out of the window, I'm the happiest woman I've ever known. I'm radiant when I step out. I hurriedly put the SIM card back in the dongle so that there's no trace of the crime. My husband calls me to bed, and I coo back to him. This is not a time to hold a grudge.

When I get back to Mangalore, I check my email. There's a message from my editor at *Outlook*. Three words: *Got it. Brilliant.*

* *

Within our marriage, my husband holds the role of People's Commissar for Labour. (At the moment he's wearing a red T-shirt and jeans. In the art-film version I'm directing in my head, I plan to dress him in the appropriate Stalinist attire.) On Sundays, we wake up late and stay in bed. In my fantasies of marriage, it is a suspended morning of making love and stepping out to eat an endless, lazy brunch. In reality, my husband goes over the events of the past week to conclude, after an elaborate analysis, that I've done practically nothing at all, and suggests a host of jobs that I should try. He usually sets himself as the stellar example.

'When I first joined the party, they sent me off to work in a garment factory. Six months in a sweatshop in Tirupur. That's where I lost the humbug of a petit bourgeois lifestyle. You need a job that will make you declass thoroughly.'

The following week, it's a job at a printing press in Mangalore. Next, it's working as a sales-girl in a showroom in the City Centre mall. The choices offered to me vary every day: candle-making factory, cashewnut packing godown.

'You'll learn the language of the people. You'll learn to live the life of working-class women. You'll then write out of experience. That will teach you how fake your feminism is. You'll not capitalize on your cunt, you will be labouring with your hands.'

I think the job of a wife comes somewhere in the middle: labouring with my cunt, labouring with my hands. As it stands, I am not sure if I am ready to take on an additional job.

* *

He is not sincere about any of these suggestions, of course. He is the type of anxious husband who stands outside the door of a toilet in a train carriage afraid that I might seize that opportunity to give him the slip, disappear into another faraway compartment, get down at a random station and vanish without a trace. He is not going to let me go to a workplace unsupervised and risk losing me. These 'declassing jobs' are just thrown in the air to catch me out. Tomorrow, he will bring up my reluctance to pack cashews as evidence of my middle-class life, as proof that I do not want to live by manual labour. Communist ideas are a cover for his own sadism.

I have stopped asking him to help me find a job. I half-promise myself that I'll still apply for a teaching position when the new semester begins, but I'm not sure I believe myself anymore. Having a job becomes one of many vague things that I want to do in my life but see little way of attaining.

Being a writer is now a matter of self-respect. It is the job title that I give myself. I realize that my husband does not hate anything in this universe as much as the idea of a writer (a petit bourgeois woman writer, at that), so I forge a sense of reverence towards the job of being a writer.

But it's not just about antagonizing him. There is a distasteful air of the outlaw that accompanies the idea of a writer in my husband's mind. A self-centredness about writing that doesn't fit with his image of a revolutionary. It has the one-word job description: defiance. I've never felt such a dangerous attraction towards anything else in my life.

* *

Back when everything around me came crashing down, when my One True Love broke my heart, I quit a full-time teaching job so that I could write, write, write. There was nothing else I wanted to do. Now, I'm reduced to a position where I've nothing else to do.

Writer. Just that, just to myself, just in front of the mirror.

I play wife, but the minute my husband walks out, I'm screaming *yes yes yes yes yes yes* in my head, and I obsess about what I need to be writing. Domestic chores do not allow me to work with deadlines. What propels me forward is my restless urge to tell a story.

It's a novel about militant resistance to feudalism and caste. The characters in my book – still half-formed, as yet unnamed – stand up against the brute force of the state machinery, against the menacing threats of landlords. They march across me. They swear by the red flag of Communism, pay with their lives.

The theme is resistance and defiance.

Can I write this novel? Will the fear in my state of mind eat into my writing? Will I be betrayed by these words I choose? How many words can you write before they turn traitors?

I find myself incapable of writing even a single word.

The women in the book I'm supposed to be writing are so strong.

I'm nothing like them. My life shames me before my prose gets a similar chance.

* *

I find poetry easier. I try to bury my anger in words. As I sit and type at my laptop, tears running down my face, I realize he is watching me intently. There is something about my act of writing a poem that disturbs him deeply. He spies the irregular lines, the paragraph breaks, the jagged lines that could only belong to a poem. The fractured page crushes him. He comes close to me, and pleads: 'No. Don't do this. Don't do this – for the sake of us, for the sake of our future. We can move away from our differences. If you put this within a poem, it will stay there, imprisoned forever. It will be a poison that will never let us move further, it will never let us forgive, or forget.'

I cannot agree with what he has to say. To me, it sounds strange, alien almost, to imagine that my poem will be the source of future trouble, that a poem will prevent us from healing. The poem is the healing, I tell him. It's by writing this that I can get over it.

He is vehemently against putting my pain into poetry. 'No, no, that is not how it works.' He is shouting at me. 'You are missing the whole point about materialism. You think that materialism is merely believing only in the things that exist. To you, materialism is one of the ways in which you defend your atheism. That is a very shallow view. I take it seriously. I believe that as long as a material basis exists to remind us of the fights and misunderstandings that we have had, we can never truly transcend these troubles. We will be held back, against our will. Do not make the temporary into something permanent. Do not make a passing emotion into an objective reality.'

That is how it happens. A permanent injunction against my poetry.

* *

This entire discourse about materialism disappears when he is the one writing poems. When I try to remind him, he turns the arguments on their pretty heads.

'Yes, I know this is material basis. Yes, I know that this will exist long after you and I have moved past this stage of fighting. I want this material to remain, to remind me of how cruel I have been, to never let me forget that I have wronged you, to make me feel truly guilty not only because I have hurt you, but also because I have forsaken my ideals, I have not behaved like a Communist.'

And how do you justify that your poems can be written, but that I cannot write poems on my marriage?

Once again, a play of words to justify the duplicity. 'Your poems blame me. My poems blame me. There is a difference between the hatred that fuels your poems, and the self-criticism that forms the backbone of mine. Your poems label me and put me in a box, my poems struggle to move past my weaknesses.'

And that is that. In this marriage in which I'm beaten, he is the poet. And one of his opening lines of verse reads:

> *When I hit you,*
> *Comrade Lenin weeps.*

I cry, he chronicles. The institution of marriage creates its own division of labour.

VI

I folded the clothes,
arranged them in the almirah,
dimmed the lights,
straightened the bedspread,
placed the two pillows side-by-side
and wore the nightie.

In front of my thirst lies
the forbidden drink of night;
with dreams that relish many tastes,
my sleep loiters outside the room.

ANAR, 'SLEEP LOITERING OUTSIDE THE ROOM'

The common, widely held opinion is that writers dig the ruins, scour the past, always put themselves there. Yes. But at strange times they put themselves elsewhere. My husband is railing at me, slapping me, throwing my laptop across the small kitchen, forcing me to delete a manuscript, a non-fiction book-in-progress, because somewhere in its pages there is a mention of the word lover. He accuses me of carrying my past into our present, and this treason is evidence enough that there is no hope or space for the future to flourish. At this point I am not listening to him. I have no intention of responding. I am thinking of being at a point in the future when I would be writing about this moment, about this fight, about the stinging slaps that mark my cheeks and only stop when I have deleted what I have written, about how I am forced into arguing about freedom of expression with the man I have married, about the man I have married with whom it has finally come to this, to this argument about the freedom of expression. And I am thinking of how I am someday going to be writing all this out and I am conscious that I am thinking about this and not about the moment, and I know that I have already escaped the present and that gives me hope, I just have to wait for this to end and I can write again, and I know that because I am going to be writing about this, I know that this is going to end.

* *

What does my husband know of love? Does deleting an email, a book-in-progress, a random user-generated reference on Wikipedia, the history of all the Bluetooth devices my phone has paired up with, delete what I have felt for someone? If the material does not exist, does the memory go away as well?

* *

I write letters to lovers I have never seen, or heard, to lovers who do not exist, to lovers I invent on a lonely morning. Open a file, write a paragraph or a page, erase before lunch. The sheer pleasure of being able to write something that my husband can never access. The revenge in writing the word lover, again and again and again. The knowledge that I can do it, that I can get away with doing it. The defiance, the spite. The eagerness to rub salt on his wounded pride, to reclaim my space, my right to write.

* *

LETTER TO A LOVER

This is not a typical love letter. I give you no news of sparrows that I spy perched outside my window, no anecdotes of the vicious fight I witnessed between two nuns who walked past my home. Today, as I begin to write to you, I want to write with gravitas, to write about things that are beyond me, beyond you, too.

I wonder how an opportunist like my husband managed to make inroads into a political party that I have always respected; how he succeeded in hoodwinking the leadership at every stage, how he came to be what he is today. For all its celebration of introspection and self-criticism, how could they not have seen him for what he is? Were they relaxed with what they saw, did they wash it all away as patriarchal, feudal tendencies that are inevitable in someone coming from a small village? Did they not notice his attitude towards women – were they fine with it, did they try to censure him, or did they themselves share the same kind of nervousness and disdain towards feminists? Was respect and love something that the radical only reserved for women who were gun-toting rebels, women who attended and applauded at every party meeting, women who distributed pamphlets and designed placards? How did these women survive these violent, aggressive men in their ranks? Did they walk out? Did they fight? Did they leave their sexuality behind or did they barter it to make life in the organization easier?

I fell in love with the man I married because when he spoke about the revolution it seemed more intense than any poetry, more moving than any beauty. I'm no longer convinced. For every genuine revolutionary in the ranks, there is a careerist, a wife-beater, an opportunist, a manipulator, an infiltrator, a go-getter, an ass-licker, an alcoholic and a dopehead. For every militant fighter who dies on the front-line, a fraud comes and claims the slain man's greatness. For every original thinker, the parrot in the ranks who claims the wisdom as his own. Parties build themselves on the shoulders of real heroes, nurture themselves on their bloodshed, even as the imposters make merry.

That is why I yearn for you.

You, without any masquerade. You, without any glorious struggle in front of you. You, just shining in your own light, dwelling in your own darkness, you, with no grand zeal. You, with only your words, and no highfalutin theory. You, who told me on a rainy morning that when you were dead you wanted to be buried in my hair. The same you, who married another girl three years later. You, with all your contradictions, you, who do not make promises, you, who do not judge. You are real, and now, I need your realness.

* *

LETTER TO A LOVER

I write to you because I can. I do not have something concrete to say. Today is one of those days without a single new thought. Everything I think about, in the end, somehow winds up back at my marriage. The oppressive heat, the ups and downs of the roads, the sugarcane that's crushed like long, breaking bones to yield the sweetest juice, stories one hears of moral police bullying teenagers in town, the deceptive orange of the local curries. All of it becomes metaphor.

I set out to write to you about something far removed from what is going on with me. I fail. I think my state is the textbook case of a trap: when you are inside a trap, thinking about other things sets you free. Simultaneously, everything that you think about reminds you of your own state of entrapment.

When something is too obvious, I think the best course of action is to pretend not to notice it at all.

* *

LETTER TO A LOVER

You know, dear love, as well as I do, that it is difficult to stay within the frame of language and not feel desire. Sexual play is endless in ancient languages. Words are constantly weighted with the meanings they carry.

Isn't that why conversations with lovers are a constant slow tease? To flirt is to give a fresh twist to each word. I make you my own by building a little hut inside each of the words that you use, and staying with you there to watch the sunsets. When you talk of shaving your three-day beard, I whisper to you how my skin smarts with the sudden sensation of being grazed. I imbue the word kiss with the idea of clandestine; I smuggle the thought of me into the word caress. You can

91

never dislodge me from each of the words I've meticulously occupied.

Marriage has ruined my romanticism, by teaching me that this thing of beauty can be made crude. Bitch. Whore. Slut. And yet, for every insult that has been flung in my face, language retains its charm.

English makes me a lover, a beloved, a poet. Tamil makes me a word huntress, it makes me a love goddess.

There is a linguistic theory that the structures of languages determine the mode of thought and behaviour of the cultures in which they are spoken. In an effort to understand my life at the moment, I have come up with its far-fetched corollary, a distant cousin of this theory: I think what you know in a language shows who you are in relation to that language. Not an instance of language shaping your worldview, but its obtuse inverse, where your worldview shapes what parts of the language you pick up. Not just: your language makes you, your language holds you prisoner to a particular way of looking at the world. But also: who you are determines what language you inhabit, the prison-house of your existence permits you only to access and wield some parts of a language.

Now in Mangalore, I know the Kannada words *eshtu*: how much; *haalu*: milk; *anda*: eggs; *namaskaram*: greetings; *neerulli*: onion; *hendathi*: wife; *illi*: here; *ahdu*: that one; *illa*: no; *saaku*: enough; *naanu nandigudda hogabekku*: I want to go to Nandigudda.

I can dig out every single word that I've uttered in Kannada. In this language, I am nothing except a housewife.

* *

LETTER TO A LOVER

Afternoons are the most unbearable time in my life as a wife. They sprawl out and fill me with dread. I have to anticipate his arrival. I have to show him solid proof that I have been busy. I am lost in restlessness, lost in time that I cannot will away, that I cannot spend. The minutes swell into formless monsters.

Afternoons are beginning to carry in their silence and their stillness the whispered suggestion of suicide. *Do it now. It will not hurt. It will be over before you realize.* A part of me is surprised to find that, after only a handful of months, I am having to play with this thought, and then, spending the rest of the time trying to fight it. I swing on a pendulum of choice. Alive. Dead. Dead. Alive. Alive. Dead. Dead. Dead. I do not know if I'm alive now. This is the kind of alive that feels dead.

And then again, there are the dead who feel alive.

A hundred yards from where I live lies the Nandigudda cemetery. When the ghosts rise and decide to stop at the first home they encounter for a glass of water, it is my door on which they knock. In the beginning, I refused them entry, but now I have allowed them in.

The most regular visitors are the plaintive four, who were all at various points Mrs 'Cyanide' Mohan. When they appear, there is no trace of their features. Each of them eloped with the same man because he promised marriage. Each of them was presented with a special powder meant for birth control. Each of them was found dead in the toilets of public bus-stands or hotels. Each of their bodies went unclaimed by parents who had no idea of the whereabouts of their daughter. Twenty, or even more women fell prey to Mohan's charms before the police begin to connect the dots. Four of them, after lying lonely at the mortuary in Mangalore, were brought to Nandigudda for their last rites. Now, they visit me, a newly-wed like them. Who, like them, rushed into marriage. A different man, a different terror, and yet, something makes them come to me. Curiosity, perhaps. Although they all met the same end, they are jealous wives, they do not talk to each other. I know this for a fact.

* *

LETTER TO A LOVER

When I am in bed with my husband, I have learnt to be still and silent. Meditative even. Control yourself, he tells me, not in the voice of a lover who does not want to wake his neighbour, but in the voice of an angry teacher. I become the woman of Indian cinema: on the screen this holy act of marital sex is shown through my bangled hand clenching the bedsheet, and this clenching will be sudden, so that it can signal to the viewer that he has taken me in a single thrust.

The Tarantino among Tamil film-makers can instead choose to show this by a close-up of my toes that curl and hold still. Otherwise sex itself will elicit no noise, and no other movement from the woman.

So much of sex is what it is because you are allowed to be yourself. This individuality – which can be anything in a lover: fierceness, clumsiness, coyness – is what makes sex different every time, this is what changes the nature of pleasure from one act to the next, from one lover to another. To play the role of the still, passive and submissive woman day after day leaves a woman in a relationship with the ceiling, not with her man. My husband lacks this kind of basic knowledge because Marx and Lenin and Mao have not explicitly written this down, and the declassing classes do not address the sexual pleasure of comrades.

I think about you and me. One of those noisy days, hotel staff in the corridor, and our first time together. You, the man who is not silencing me, shutting me up, letting me shout. For a second that will be everything I want from this world. A moon landing of sorts. As if I finally have the permit to be myself. Like someone stamping my passport and saying, yes, you are free to visit this land, free to shout all you can, all you want. I am not sure we have met. I do not think you know that I exist.

Trust me, love, you will.

* *

As I write to my unseen, as yet undiscovered lovers, the words of my One True Love come to me. His words, with the cadences of his persuasive public speeches, smuggle me back into his arms.

My heart is on a hartal today: no traffic, everything is suspended, all shutters are down, people are staying within their homes. Only you have the unwritten permission to stroll my streets, you can dance if you wanted and sing if you cared, but love, you do not even open your window to look at me. Somewhere in the middle of this, buses are being torched, showroom windows are being shattered, police are being pressed into action, there are slogans and banners and marches, but nothing ruffles you. I make all the noise in the world, but I am alone.

You do not send me messages, not even the fragments of poems, you do not ask if I am alive. I miss you. To see if I can catch your scent, or spot the silhouette of anyone who reminds me of you, I open a window. From where I am, I do not see people, I see the sky and I watch clouds build bridges with one another – they are huge, they are slow-moving in this crude summer – but they manage to get together quicker than we do. I shut the window in disappointment, I turn the lights out, but you do

not come to me. You leave me to my loneliness. You
are cruel. I lie in wait for you. There is only stillness,
a silence fractured by the music I turn on from time
to time. I am patient, I look for the smallest sign
of you. Instead, I grow old waiting for you. You,
who said to me that love was like adoption, have
abandoned me.

I could take my life and you would only come
to know of it from the evening news, or tomorrow's
papers. I could mutilate myself, and bleed, and you
would not even know, you will not weep because
you do not know, you will not plead with me to stop
because you do not know, you will not hold my hand
with your nervous fingers, you will not comfort me
with your kisses, you will not burst into tears as you
see me hurting; nothing will happen because you are
elsewhere, my love.

I am at home, lying down on my marital bed and this is how I
sin. Memory transcribing the words of a love from long ago.
This will be a thought-crime in my husband's eyes. I do not
feel any guilt. I do not think any of his beatings or belt lash-
ings will cause me to feel any guilt. With me, at this moment, I
feel only the relish of rebellion, the comfort of long-forgotten
words that now make me feel safe, feel loved.

* *

LETTER TO A LOVER

How do I want you to imagine me as I write this to you? Not as a woman with shining eyes furiously typing away something on a laptop, a something which she will erase as evening begins to stalk her doorstep. That's the image of a wife as a writer, but I'm not a writer except in these brief snatches of time. So, you now mentally recompose the scene of me. But please don't choose one of a battered wife – that's an image that will brand itself on your mind, and the longer you think of it, the more impossible it will become for you to relate to me, to love me naturally. You will then love me like a scar loves a wound and I deserve something more.

For now, imagine me in this kitchen. The kitchen is the tiniest space in our house, but it is a space of peace. While everything about me drives him into fits of rage, it is my food that manages to placate him. It is the only redeemable thing that he finds in me. This is the something on which I can try to build, try to trick myself into the make-believe of a happy marriage. In the kitchen, I discover my mustard-grain of faith. The only ceasefire comes from the food I make. The only conversations we have where he does not begin to suspect me are when we are talking about meals. Were you to tell this story, shoot this as a culinary Bildungsroman. Include flashbacks to pine forests and orange plantations. Choose a tall, lanky thirty-year-old to play the role of a Naxalite guerrilla, struggling to eat a decent meal when he is underground, part of a twelve-member armed squad surviving in inhospitable conditions. After an experience like that, it is understandable why he is particular about taste. That is why he loves my food. Even though he interferes, and lectures me on how to reduce wastage and how to save cooking time, the kitchen is the only place in which he defers to me. It is the only component of our marriage where I have the upper hand.

Remember, lover, if you ever direct the film of my life, that the food must overshadow the domestic players. The assault on your senses will be the footage of red tomatoes breaking down in the frying pan with green chillies and pink-white onions. The tang of tamarind infusing a chicken curry turns it a rich shade of brown. The stark green of cluster beans interrupted by the brown-black of mustard seeds and the white of roasted, powdered rice. The julienned white insides of a banana stem, soaked in buttermilk, drained and then sautéed with cumin, grated coconut, a pinch of turmeric and red chilli flakes bring to your plate the lush richness of a far-away hometown. The sounds of oil sizzling as sweet-smelling cloves and cinnamon bark and fenugreek and star anise are dropped into the pan one after another. Flying white ants from a monsoon evening will be craftily trapped to make an unexpected evening snack. And here, as all these elaborate banquets are staged, you will see the picture of domestic bliss that my husband is trying hard to forge. You will see how eagerly I step into the shoes of the good housewife.

But I have learnt that food could give away my secrets. I make for my husband only the food I learnt to make from my father. I do not experiment. I do not replicate what I did with my lovers, or what I plan to do with you. Every day, I serve food to him as if it were a declaration of chastity.

* *

LETTER TO A LOVER

Yesterday, I thought about all kinds of men: the thin, the tall, the fair, the swarthy, the agile, the self-possessed and whatever else can be left to my dirty imagination. For three hours last night, I was being held hostage by my husband who sermonized on the role of clothes. 'When class disappears, the masculine and feminine disappear. Class society gives rise to the concept of shame. When shame disappears, we will all be naked.'

At first, the parade of men filing through my brain was simply a distraction from my tedious husband. But the more he droned on – 'A classless society will be a nude society. The sexualization of the naked body is a result of market forces.' – the more I took perverse delight in taking full advantage of those men in my mind.

All of this highfalutin theory about nudity was distilled hypocrisy. I knew how much my husband controlled my clothes, something I made the mistake of reporting to my mother. Love is in the little things, she said on the phone.

Wear what pleases him. Don't stand your ground or sweat yourself on the small stuff. Men are insecure about beauty. They will want to hide it in you, and then, they will take their crippled minds to town and eye-fuck every girl they see.

I'm sorry, mother dear, but I disagree. Clothes shouldn't be a battleground. They shouldn't be about control and mortification. To me, they are about the way men undress themselves – always the joy of watching a lover's awkwardness when he hurriedly removes his shirt, first the left sleeve and then the rest of it pulled up from the neck. It is the easy way women dress and undress in front of each other, our clothes made for the hands of our friends, the zip that runs along the length of the dress, the bra hook, the sari pleats at the back, as if we become complete only when we take part in dressing each other. From me, you will only hear about clothes as things that we wanted to shed, clothes that remind us of the time we were lovers. The scarf you bought for me from your visit to the Middle East which I did not ask you to show me for fear that it would mean I cared about what you felt for me, that I did not take from you for fear that it would force you to feel bad later on, the scarf an evidence of love and at once a false hope of commitment. The wine-red halter-neck I left behind in your apartment, with its little balcony and a bedroom with a cobalt blue bedspread and white curtains, as if by leaving something behind, I hoped I would have to come to you again, and then, this scarf would lie in wait for me, and we would dissolve our nights in poetry and politics and all the worst jokes in the world.

* *

LETTER TO A LOVER

I write this letter to you knowing that you will be deeply upset when you encounter Derrida's name. You will call him a wanker – the most British insult you can find in that French accent of yours. To prove to me that you can do a better job of obscurantism, you will put pen to paper and send up seven sentences that cannot be deciphered by the best minds in the world. No, we are not setting the stage for that. This is not a trap of any kind. This is about another writer, Derrida calls her the best writer in the French language, and for that reason alone, it must interest you.

I read *Hyperdream* by Hélène Cixous. There is a sentence that I hear forever, a sentence that wraps itself around an action, a sentence that travels around the life of a woman and her contemplation of pain and survival even as this woman is applying a balm of some sort to her mother's skin, and I know this is how the words sink in, in circles, smoothly cajoled into the body, into the sore spots, into the bloodstream itself. This I can write an analysis of for forty-five pages; this one winding sentence can help me put forward an example of the feminine sentence; this can help me present a paper in some conference; but most of all, this sentence has altered me already, made me look at my mother's dark skin in a new light. I imagine this skin you see, so written about, as a rose-tinted white with a hint of straw.

In Cixous's novel, there is a skin problem. In my world, skin is the problem. No Jacques Derrida would ever be blurbing me, not for all the telephone intimacy, not for all the woman on woman action in the world. Our skin doesn't let in light, there is no translucence of reflected glory, and dark women like me have a hard time bursting into intellectual, feminist scenes. Unless we turn into the soft-spoken token women hand-picked to entertain all-white audiences waiting to be bedazzled. I cannot compete with her, not now, not yet, not ever.

I love Cixous, almost want to call her Hélène on a first-name basis in my fantasy thesis, but I become dismissive of this novel, this hyperdream. The French, which has seeped into the translation, is perhaps the saving grace. Those italicized words in this language, of a power that did not colonize my land even as it ravaged others, perhaps hold the key. If given a chance, it is those French words – unambiguous, unlike, say, the adverb *encore* – that must explain and contain my howling rage at language, at literature, at everything that is flawed and twisted.

And then, after an endless number of pages, I find something.

Dieu n'a pas d'yeux.

God has no eyes.

That line is a kick to the gut. Indeed, God has not seen the smile on a little girl's face the first time her palms eclipse the sun, nor has he seen the tears of a battered wife as she thinks of her unborn children.

* *

LETTER TO A LOVER

This is the letter that I have been writing to you for days. Living in Mangalore, where rain trespasses into every private sphere, how do I reduce the rain for you?

The abandoned clothes pegs are getting wet, holding ear-lobes of water. Fuchsia. Aquamarine. Fuchsia. Aquamarine. Fuchsia again. I loved them as a child, clipping one clothes peg to the ear of another, until they were long enough to trail after me through the house, a caravan of clothes pegs, and to adorn me, a daisy-chain garland of gem clips, with precise colour repetitions. In a marriage, there's no such room to fool around. Everything has form and function. Everything belongs in its place. The peg on the clothesline, the gem clips on the table, the coat-hanger in the closet, the woman in the kitchen, the submissive between the sheets.

I open the doors to step outside and watch the unending ropes of rain. It is the relief and the respite that I seek from the sultriness of staying locked in. It is this rain that comes to me carrying the scent of long-ago lovers. In rain, I hide my memories of happier days. In rain, I chant the names of men I want. In rain, my body responds to me, loses its restraint, forgets the decorum required of good women. In rain, I hide the shame of the unexplained wetness between my legs. In rain, I drown out the silence in my blood. In rain, I absolve myself of guilt: I am wife, I am chained to this fate, I have made peace with life. It is this rain that tells me to run away in every way it can, rain that comprehends my misery, rain that fills me with sadness and longing, rain that sows the seeds of discord, rain that sends me into irrevocable silences, rain that informs this letter I write.

* *

Each of my letters, I delete after I have finished typing them. Every line I have written to you is a thought-crime, a crime that does not leave a trail of evidence, a crime that is not even a crime. If my husband was to ever ask me about this, I plan to use his own line of reasoning: There is no material basis here, so what do you want me to do?

VII

Old lovers go the way of old photographs, bleaching out gradually as in a slow bath of acid: first the moles and pimples, then the shadings. Then the faces themselves, until nothing remains but the general outlines.

MARGARET ATWOOD, CAT'S EYE

There is always a clumsy first time, which is often forgotten for the purposes of history, but remembered in the service of nostalgia, and recounted under duress from demanding husbands.

This happened long ago. This happened before I was aware of things like remembering and forgetting. This happened in circumstances where I could not talk about it though I was in the centre of it.

* *

I am twenty-something, he is approaching forty. I am a student, a migrant, with nothing to call my own here. I speak a smattering of Malayalam, in every word I utter my native Tamil peeks through; the vernacular media in Kerala calls him the greatest orator of his generation. He is the most charismatic politician in the state, the grandson of a revolutionary, the darling of the regional press, the lone crusader, the insider who is dismantling a corrupt system, the dedicated young man who will change the country.

This man is all the men I had been looking for.

* *

We almost always met in secret.

The happiness at seeing each other, overshadowed by our sadness at having to meet in this manner. Time, cupped in the palms of our hands, as if to prevent its spillage. Afraid to let go, afraid to rush through. Afraid that a little less impatience in the beginning, a little hurry towards the end, would be the beginning of the end. Breathless with anticipation. Breathing heavily, burdened by the heaviness of our secret, by the years that separate us in the eyes of the world. And any void in conversation, filled in by reciting the half-remembered, half-forgotten lines of poems. Laughing at each other's jokes. Speaking in elaborate riddle. Embattled love, reckless embraces, coupled with the shamelessness of perfect strangers.

Some days, the awkwardness of expressing our physical hungers.

Some nights, intimacies dished out with the freshness of first love.

In the backdrop, the many incessant trademarks of a lover's quarrel.

Fighting about who loved whom more.

Fighting about our fighting.

Giving each other names.

Fucking, without giving a fuck.

There was a lot of kissing. There was the blood and bones, the smell of sex and aftershave, the beauty that kept us going. There was, what could only be called, love.

* *

Things move quickly. Before I realize it, I am doing little things for him. One moment, I'm coordinating his interview with a foreign journalist, another, I'm proofreading the draft of a press release he has hurriedly emailed me. A week later, I'm researching for a speech he has to make at a university in another state. An inaugural keynote address on the role of the state machinery during communal riots. I walk around with Omar Khalidi's slim new book, download numerous PDFs, cut out newspaper editorials, find reports of Police Commissions that indict the force for its non-neutrality. I try to put together a speech knowing that he would not read it aloud, that he would probably speak extempore, that his gift of the gab would be better than any words I write for him.

Knowing him, he would be talking a great deal about the Beemapalli police shootings, as the police had no right to enter that tiny seaside town and shoot down five Muslim men. It is a story of the state making the minorities an easy prey for its own excesses. The mainstream media and the civil society have looked the other way, but my man is one of the few who has raised his voice to break the silence. His press conferences, his media interviews, his memorandums, his demonstrations have all revolved around this issue for the last three months. I do the research because he asked for it, despite knowing that he has an army of people at his command to do this sort of thing: retired professors, ex-classmates, upcoming journalists, young men with documentation jobs in NGOs, young women in academia with political science degrees, the standard-issue types of people who would be happy to jump at a chance to help, happy to throw themselves at his service. Sometimes, it appears to me as if I am doing all this work to keep the competition out. I have no role, no position, no connection to his party. All of my engagement stems from the fact that I'm in love with him. Lost in romance, I savour these errands that come my way.

To myself, I reason that these tasks are his way of finding a chance to spend time with me: text messages, long phone calls, an unannounced secret visit to my office. I know that this work is beyond work, it is beyond politics, beyond the deadline and the word-count. When I am assigned to do something for him I think that this is how our love renews itself, constantly seeking to be on the same page, sharing common ground. It is like the way in which he says at the end of every call: 'I will talk to you later', 'I will talk to you to-night', 'I will call you first thing in the morning' as if we were engaged in one unceasing conversation, and when we find ourselves interrupted, we simply pause, ready and waiting to pick it up again right from where we had left off.

* *

Some nights, our phone conversations become an endless catalogue of his health problems. It crushes me that I am not with him; that I cannot do anything to comfort him. On the phone with him, all I have is the night sky that carries his thousand eyes. And there, the moon with a bellyache, the moon with a back pain, the moon with a bleeding heart, the moon in which I see all his moods.

All this travel has given me a constant backache.

Eating hotel food, eating out-of-hours, not eating at all – everything is aggravating my ulcer.

My forehead was burning hot this afternoon, and now I am wrapped in a blanket to stop the chills; I think Kochi's mosquitoes have given me malaria again. Yes, I will see a doctor tomorrow.

My feet are swollen, my big toe is numb, could it mean a serious nervous problem? The MRI scan this January did not show anything out of the ordinary. Maybe I need a second opinion?

I have lost my voice, this is what the campaign trail does to you. It is three days since I slept; unscheduled events are killing me. I no longer have a life that functions according to plan.

The boy who does the massage did not turn up this week.

I am thinking about a full-body-health check-up.

The 'glass of green tea every hour' idea is good, but it ruins my appetite.

It is the stress, nothing else.

I am worlds removed from medicine, but I listen. He is not a hypochondriac, but he seems to have more health problems than my mother and her friends combined. The talk about illness becomes so central to his everyday, that now, almost out of habit, I work it into our conversations; I inquire about his state of health every time we call each other. I do not know how or why it has come to this. I think, in one of my fanciful theories that seeks to explain and preserve everything around me, that this is one of the ways in which he shows his trust in me, exposing himself at his weakest, divulging his frailties, sharing with me the sorrows of his unforgiving flesh, perhaps warning me that life with an older man comes with complications, perhaps preparing me for a lifetime with him.

He might be a strong, invincible man to the world outside, but to me, he is someone in need of tenderness. I sometimes read this as a plea for sympathy: as if pitying him would make me love him more, and by extension, my fierce love would protect him from the torment of tiredness and routine illness.

Maybe he does not harbour the same romantic illusions. For him, this is an intimacy he can easily afford – an intimacy that does not promise commitment, an intimacy that will not be judged.

Health complications might just be the other, unglamorous, matter-of-fact side of his life – getting off at a random railway station, meeting the first doctor around the corner, baring his buttocks to a shy nurse for a shot of diclofenac, downing a cocktail of medicines to keep himself going, to turn up in small towns to address meetings on promised dates.

* *

In love, I inhabit an imaginary underground; I simultaneously exist and do not exist. I'm summoned into being when my lover needs me; I'm dismissed, like a genie sent back to its bottle, when he is done with me.

I have made a temporary peace with this arrangement, as the world does not know of our untitled, unclaimed love.

Some know that I am his friend, but no one knows for sure whether I am his lover. They tell me salacious stories about him and then watch intently for my reaction. A twitch. A blush. A tell-tale sign. I remain impassive. I restrain the urge to feed their curiosity.

Those moments that I share with him, I keep them to myself. But the stories I hear, I do not always manage to throw to the wind. They stick with me, they stalk me. These stories sow the seeds of doubt. I begin to live in them. I look for evidence to believe them. When it becomes difficult to dismiss them as groundless gossip, I confront him. It is unpleasant and painful. Like cutting into my own flesh with a blade. Like taking someone captive. It breaks the languid charm of our relationship – that space without fights, that absence of raised voices, that snuggle-area we have fashioned for ourselves, where hurt does not enter, or exist.

It leaves us in a zone of discomfort. When doubt raises its multiple heads, the elements of love falter. To ask a man if a rumour about him is true comes with its own consequences: 'You are suspicious. You do not trust me. Where there is no trust, there is no love.'

I disclose to him that I heard of his dalliance with an actress. I report back to him, in excruciating detail, after a journalist calls me up to inform me that my lover's stopover in Singapore had something more to it. One of my friends says he is supporting an upcoming academic because they share a bed as well as political passion, and the day I run into her in his office, I freeze, I cannot find words, I cannot smile, I cannot stay in her presence. I do not believe every story that comes my way, I know that some of it is dubious. But I cannot always contain myself, I bring it up despite my best efforts. These rumours that are passed on to me hunker down in the trenches of my mind, ready to charge when I feel neglected. It does not unsettle him. He dismisses it as the handiwork of his detractors – the occupational hazard of being a politician.

I believe him. I bring myself to believe that there can be smoke without fire, even if that smoke blinds me and makes my eyes stream with tears.

In truth, it is a simple story.

I had set out to love a man who loved people. Instead, I found myself with a man who loved women.

* *

Advice to young women who are into hero-worship: the world is full of women in love with the men who you are in love with.

Learn to live with that.

* *

Whenever I visit his office, whether I go there with a journalist or student or with a woman whose rape complaint has been ignored by the police, or a construction worker hunted by the local loan shark, or just because I want to steal a look at him, a hush settles on the men around him. There is a forced cordiality that masks their discomfort. They enact a fake amiability – greet me, ask about my health, how work is going and if I have found a job. The cocky ones among them inevitably tease me – joking that I plan to run for an MLA election in the future, that I am gunning for the post of the party's media secretary, or the women's wing, or the students' wing, or whatever comes to their mind at that moment. Sized up, measured, put down: this is the fate that befalls those of us who are not political heirs.

I am unlike any of the notable women in politics: daughter-in-law of a former chief minister, younger sister of a home minister, wife of a political bigwig convicted in the teachers recruitment scam, wife of a party ex-president, the widow of the students' wing secretary who was brutally murdered, the daughter of a caste leader who had recently defected from one party to another. What they have is what I lack – the family steeped in politics. Fathers to build me, brothers to prop me up, uncles to launch me into their media empires. It is clear as day that the only way in which I will be a legitimate part of the political circus will be through marriage.

And so, for this reason alone, I detest the idea of marriage, the idea that it would be perceived as a means to an end, the idea that becoming a wife would be read as ambition rather than love. But politics is primitive, and I know that this is the settled practice through which an outsider may join the tribe.

I have not yet been anointed as wife. And although the gossip abounds, no one has a clue what our relationship is and what my intentions are. To his cadre who make jokes about my ambition, I counter with sharp retorts: 'So is that the post you want for yourself, *chetta*? I will put in a word for you.' And to those who suggest a love affair, I get away by saying: 'Oh no. I love him the way one loves a leader. My love for him is no different than your love for him, *chetta*.' Such repartee does not change anyone's opinion. It only makes it easier for me to put on a brave, indifferent face. To these pur-pose-hunters of love, no answer will ever be good enough.

* *

Marriage is not the first thing on my to-do list. It is not the end of the road, the culmination of love. I make this clear, I do not mince my words.

'I do not ask you to marry me because I love you and you love me. I do not ask for you to marry me because this is the thing that people in love do. I do not ask you to marry me be-cause I believe in marriage or because I believe in this society. I do not ask you to marry me because we can live together night and day or because I would die if I do not get to wash your underwear with my own delicate hands. I do not ask you to marry me because I want to be your dazzling trophy wife, or because I can be the gold-digger who married up, up, up above her status.

'I want you to marry me because I want to confront the reasons why you refuse to marry me. When you fail to take even a step towards marriage, I want to know why this idea does not exist on your horizon. I want to know why I am rejected even if you never say these words yourself. I want to know what it is about me that makes me unworthy of being your wife.

'I want to know if I was another woman – richer, fairer, less educated or more buxom, an industrialist's daughter, an MP's sister – if I would be given the stamp of approval.'

'This is the kind of feminism that ruins love,' he replies. 'This manner in which you frame it, the way in which you demand marriage as a right, instead of looking at it as the next logical location where our love would take us. This is the feminism that calculates,' he says, 'the feminism that negotiates, the feminism with a balance sheet. This is not love that waits. This is not a love that has wrapped itself in trust and therefore cannot, ever, feel doubt.

'The problem is your feminism, your feminism that makes you an individual, the feminism that refuses to recognize that we are a couple, the feminism that makes you build a barricade all around yourself, the feminism that sows the seeds of distrust in your mind about me because it cannot see me as anything other than a man and men as anything other than selfish scoundrels.

'If you are a woman in love, and I am the man you love, aren't we a unit of ourselves, one together, the one living in two? Would I not have your interests in my heart? Would I not see you as I see myself? How do you treat me as another? How do you even think that I could betray you? Why do you situate yourself outside the couple and alienate me? Why do you hound me with these questions? Your feminism is killing our love. And, just so you know, I am not the problem. I am not the problem and you know that. You are not the problem either. Your feminism is.'

I listen in silence.

'Your feminism will drive away all the men who come your way. No man stands a chance.'

* *

I watch love transform. Alone in his office, his hands find my breasts, he crushes me in his hasty embrace, he kisses my cheeks, my eyelids, he settles upon my lips and, in a minute of stolen intimacy, ends this in a hug where his hardness declares itself to me against my thigh. Then, the rhythm of the approaching footsteps in the corridor makes us retreat into our old, familiar positions – him on his throne behind the desk, me in front like a supplicant. There, he sharpens up, his eyes narrow, his lips pucker into contemplativeness, he runs his fingers over his moustache. He makes a wry observation. In the presence of a third person his love is programmed to self-destruct.

I cannot match my politician. I sit there, my heart pounding, my fingers fidgeting, a light in my eyes that refuse to dim, in a state of excitement that does not subside.

* *

Let me tell you something that goes against popular wisdom.

Love is not blind; it just looks in the wrong places.

* *

First love forges a different woman out of me. It tires me with responsibility. Fighting for my love to sustain itself, for it to be given a name, a suitable face and necessary public history, I am jolted awake from the reverie-landscape of lovers. If love is a place marked by the absence of questions, I'm no longer there. I have left with questions. I am left with questions.

As it is their nature, questions between lovers can deteriorate into accusations.

It is no longer: What will become of me?

Or: What does the future hold for us?

Or: What shall we do with our lives?

This is the end of open-ended questions. An interrogative becomes a declarative. A sentiment becomes a charge-sheet. A statement becomes a sentence.

'You used me.'

Another man in his place would have declared his love all over again, made peace and a promise of marriage. He merely turns feminist.

'Why do you think I "used" you? Is this how you reduce our love: into a one-way street? Did you not have any role, any control in what happened? This is downright dirty. Your thinking is cheap and problematic. I did not "use" you. Not anymore than you "used" me. If you think you "lost" something by sleeping with me, then remember that I lost the same thing by sleeping with you. I think you are saying this in anger. You do not mean it, my love. You cannot have such a low opinion of me, or such a low opinion of sex. Do not look at it that way: me "using" you; no, we, the two of us, we "shared" something.'

I do not know what to say. I'm just about half his age, but even I can see that he only adopts this convenient Feminist Dialectic because he will never commit to me. With these dispassionate arguments, I see us lose the poetry that holds us together.

* *

It seemed as if the people of our nation had decided – or, as if it had been decided on behalf of the people of our nation – that the only way to counter the political narrative of 'dynasty' was to spin the opposite narrative of 'bachelorhood'. A man free of a visible woman would be free of visible progeny who would lay claim to his legacy. Maybe it was meant to signal that, having no heirs, these men would have no impulse to be corrupt, to amass wealth, to build dynasties. Maybe it meant that not having any domestic responsibilities, these men would devote all their time to the service of society. These bachelor politicians emerged in every tiny village and every tiny ward-councillor election – flaunting the absence of a family.

The original and most popular bachelor politician was of course Gandhi, the goat-milk-drinking-groundnut-eating Gandhi, the father-of-the-nation Gandhi. Gandhi was a married man who managed the miracle of becoming a bachelor politician. He made his celibacy public. This gave him a sainthood, whereas anywhere else in the world he would have been berated or mocked for denying pleasure to his wife and for not taking his conjugal responsibilities seriously. He also floated the rumour that the loss of semen equalled the loss of energy, which sent the nation into orgiastic repression. To ejaculate was to emasculate. No man wanted to lose his power and his potency having sex. A woman by your side meant that you were not masculine enough, not man enough to lead the people. So, when they had the chance, the men who could not stick with celibacy (unlike Gandhi) decided to hide the women they were with, so that they could continue to remain bachelor politicians.

Atal Bihari Vajpayee – with an adopted daughter, and a live-in partner, Mrs Kaul – was a bachelor politician. Narendra Modi – with a wife he managed to abandon and purge from our collective memory, even as he had his hands full with launching an anti-Muslim pogrom – was another.

So is the man I am with: Bachelor. Politician.

This label makes him stand out. This label conveys the pledge that his life is dedicated to serving the people. This label conveys that he takes his semen seriously. How can I stake a claim without making him lose this label? How can I press for marriage if he keeps declaring that it would prove costly to his political life? How can I step out of the shadows, and bring our love to light, knowing in advance that it would be catastrophic to his career?

To keep this love, I have to keep it secret, I have to whip myself into becoming secret. When I cease being the secret, perhaps I will cease being his lover.

* *

In a sense, he is my secret too.

He is the reason why I stay back in Kerala even after my master's degree, why I settle for a measly salary in a charitable Christian college in a contract-based teaching job, and why I vehemently shut down any marriage proposals to the sons of neighbours and the brothers of friends that my eager family puts forward.

They do not know of the existence of a lover in my life. My mother thinks that I am one of those women who get so deep into English literature that my only love will ever be for Shakespeare and my only passion and pleasure will ever be from the thrust of iambic pentameter. My father, with his evergreen ambitious outlook on life, imagines that I have remained in Kerala because it will open the door for me to find teaching opportunities in the Middle East and I will soon be making hefty remittances home in dirhams and dinars and riyals.

I cannot tell them about the politician yet. His unwilling-
ness to marry me makes it impossible for me even to broach
the topic. I have lived with my parents long enough to know
that they will dismiss the whole love affair as fooling around
and frivolous sex.

Tired of living in denial, one day I try the ancient method
of testing the waters. I take tried-and-tested refuge in speaking of a friend who has started seeing a politician who's much
older than her. My mother has a panic attack on the phone:
cut all contact with this girl and keep away from trouble and
what is wrong with young women of your age do you not
know that politicians are hoodlums and rapists who will carry
you away and one day you are going to find your friend dead
in an abandoned outhouse or this man is going to prostitute
her to other politicians and oh good lord stay away from all
this and do not ever meet this monster because today he is
after your friend but tomorrow he will want you in bed as
well and if you end up dead the news will not even reach us
because we live so far away. Relax, Mom, relax relax relax. I
have a hard time changing the topic. I assure her that I will
make sure that I never cross paths with a politician in my life.
After that phone call, I never mention this friend again.

* *

Secrecy is cancerous – it begins to eat us from the inside.
The necessity to keep our love under wraps feeds our fear of

losing each other, the fear of losing a life together. Intimacy is replaced by our fear of fear, a fear of evenings, a fear of lonely nights, his fear of gossip taking to the streets, my fear of being misunderstood. One day, we are waiting for someone to re-arrange the stars so that our fates change, and another day, we are waiting for the axe to fall and cleave us apart. I watch him chase his privacy like a little animal scurrying away to hide from a storm. I watch him, within our safe zone, love with a flamboyance beyond my imagination. One day, the wind may change direction – we may be left together, or we may be uprooted, torn asunder, thrown across different worlds. Not knowing breaks us. Knowing would break us too.

* *

The end comes at an unexpected moment.

The hospital ward resembles a village fair: his friends, his cadres, his relatives, media persons and his retinue of lady admirers – thoroughly sanitized by respectable marriages – are all present. Everyone is streaming in and out. I encounter them in the little tea-stall outside the hospital, in the reception area, in the corridor, in the queue waiting for the lifts, en route to his room. Everyone seems to have known of his emergency admission to the hospital, everyone seems to have known where to go to meet him. Everyone, with the exception of me.

I had tried in vain to reach him over the phone the previous evening and night. I had frantically called his secretary and driver – and they had given me evasive answers, reluctant to say anything. This morning, his media liaison, taking pity on me, had called me to the hospital.

I'm hysterical, in tears, not knowing what happened to him. I'm the last of his extended circle to get there. I find every eye pinned on me. There are hushed whispers that I choose to ignore. In their presence, my politician-lover treats me like a perfect stranger. He makes polite enquiries, not for a moment showing any sign that he had spent the last afternoon in bed with me. I'm dying to hold his hand, to go and kiss his feverish forehead, to stay by his bedside till he recovers. I cannot do any of that because it would be deemed inappropriate. When I try to take a step forward, so that I'm allowed to get a little closer to him, he turns me away with a quick sweeping glance.

A few minutes later, the doctor enters and all of us leave the room.

That is the last I see of him.

I decide against a love that decides against acknowledging me. I want a man for whom I will have the right to mourn in public, by whose dead body I can sit for the last few hours before it is consigned to ashes, on whom I can throw myself and weep my heart to a stop. This is not feminism.

I am just a woman in love.

VIII

He was a perfect husband: he never picked up anything from the floor, or turned out a light, or closed a door.

GABRIEL GARCÍA MARQUÉZ,
LOVE IN THE TIME OF CHOLERA

My husband is in the kitchen.

He is channelling his anger, practising his outrage. I am the wooden cutting board banged against the countertop. I am the clattering plates flung into the cupboards. I am the unwashed glass being thrown to the floor. Shatter and shards and diamond sparkle of tiny pieces. My hips and thighs and breasts and buttocks. Irreversible crashing sounds, a fragile sight of brokenness as a petty tyrant indulges in a power-trip. Not for the first time, and not for the last.

I hold back tears. I will not become a traitor to my cause. Tomorrow, the clean-up is going to be all mine. He continues smashing things. Try harder, husband. Try harder. I am not going to be tamed by these tantrums.

* *

one two
tame the shrew
one two
just push through
one two
yes thank you

* *

We are supposed to go to a protest meeting.

I'm getting dressed. It's the first time I'm leaving home in two weeks, so I wear kohl and a touch of lipstick.

'Don't expect that you will one day earn the trust of the working-class women if you strut around with your lipstick and handbag. They will mistake you for a prostitute.'

'Is the prostitute not a working woman?'

I knew it was coming; I knew I had tempted fate, but I just couldn't resist. He flies into a rage, tearing my bag from my shoulder and hurling it against the wall.

'Not a prostitute like you, not a petit-bourgeois prostitute like you. Under Communism there will be no prostitution. Under Communism, a petit-bourgeois woman like you will have to give up her petit-bourgeois privileges. The lipstick will not survive the New Democratic Revolution. The lipstick that costs three hundred rupees is not something that society needs. The lipstick that is more than the weekly wage of a tribal woman in Chhattisgarh exists only because it allows petit-bourgeois bitches to send the signal that they are on heat and ready to barter their sexual availability in exchange for favours. The lipstick is a symbol of this transaction and this availability, there is nothing beautiful about it.'

I am on the verge of tears; he sees this and, fearing that we'll be late for the meeting, he changes his tone. He begins to pacify me, begins to pull out other reasons to support his anti-lipstick crusade. He tells me I am the victim of a cosmetics industry trying to sell me back the confidence it has stolen from me. He tells me that I am a very beautiful woman and that I do not need anything to be added to my face, least of all anything that capitalism has decreed as good. Knowing that this berating and patronizing will never cease, I throw my lipstick in the bin. I rub off the purple of my lips on my *dupatta*. This temporarily shuts him up. He appears smug and triumphant. We leave for the protest: two perfect comrades. The revolution is just around the corner.

* *

That night, he prepares the bed, plumps the pillows, and calls me to join him. I'm doing the last of the dinner dishes, watching the clear moon from the window. He calls me again, a note of irritation in his voice. I wash the last dish and wave goodbye to the moon, who watches me leave before turning her gaze to the graveyard next door, where the newly buried dead sleep away their deferred dreams, the finicky dead rejoice in a rainless night, the friendly dead squat in a circle and tell each other stories, the silent dead soak in the faint white light, and the melancholic dead think of loved ones they have left behind. The moon has a difficult job cut out for her night after night.

* *

Another day, another story. Now, the scene shifts outside the four walls of our house. The claustrophobia that I feel must not infect the entire narrative. Sometimes, to step outside is to achieve breathing space.

It's nearly eleven o'clock. We're leaving Chef Xinlai in Attavar, satisfyingly full of dumplings and egg drop soup, Singapore fried rice and chow mein. We're holding hands. He looks happy, a little protective, even. I secretly wish we had more evenings out like this one. Good food that gives me a break from cooking. Getting away from our house to explore the town. The calm drowsiness we feel as we walk this long stretch back home in pitch darkness broken only by the lights of an occasional speeding motorbike or the glow from the *kulfi* shops that stay open at night.

He remarks about how I'm more attuned to walking since I married him. It sounds like a compliment. He says it's a sign of my giving up the perks of middle-class life. I grew up in a forest, I tell him. We went for walks every day.

'Your parents have a car.'

'They bought it on a loan last year. My mom had to work twenty-five years in the same job to be able to afford one.'

'You don't know what it is to walk as a poor person.'

'And you do?'

He's silent for a moment. And then he snarls at me in the dark.

'Nothing about you has changed, has it? I was a fucking fighter. Ordering *chow mein* is the closest your cunt has got to Maoism.'

* *

I'm a blinking red dot lying flat at the bottom left of a large, flat-screen monitor. The screen is blank except for a red star at the top right. Every time my husband gives me an orientation course about the revolution or a lesson in declassing, this red dot inches diagonally up the screen. This is my cunt moving closer to Maoism. The red dot fades to purple when it is undergoing a crash course in political economy. The red dot turns black during a session on self-criticism. The red dot turns white when it is in the process of learning. Whenever there is a slight move towards the star, the red dot flashes. This is accompanied by the sound of the same computer-generated applause that comes at the end of a game of Solitaire.

I'm curious to find out what the red dot will do on a red letter day. My birthday.

At the stroke of midnight, my mother calls to wish me many happy returns. My father won't wish me happy returns, however, as he is unhappy himself: he thinks I'm not doing enough to make the marriage work, so he won't come to the phone. I hear my mother pleading with him, but it is met by silence. She asks to speak to my husband, they exchange a few polite words, and then she hangs up.

He stands there looking at me, before wrapping me up in an awkward hug. 'Happy birthday,' he whispers. This is my first birthday with him. I'm turning twenty-seven.

He fetches a fruitcake from the fridge and I find myself oddly touched.

I cut us both a slice and we eat in silence. When he swallows the last of his cake, he takes my hand in his.

'I've made a compromise.'

'By marrying me?'

'No. By celebrating your birthday.'

'But I didn't ask you to.'

'Yes. But you are used to it. It's a middle-class girl thing. To make a big fuss about the day they were born.'

'But you didn't marry middle-class girls. You married me.'

He abruptly drops my hand. 'It's these tiny compromises that erode me. It's why I'm a married man today, instead of being a militant. I'm a salaried dog, instead of being underground. That's the petit-bourgeois vacillation that Mao talks about.'

I am taken aback by the sudden, intense turn of conversation. I try to lighten the mood.

'I'll try harder. Tell me, what does a true Communist do on his birthday, then?'

'I observe my birthday on the day of martyrdom of Bhagat

Singh. 23 March. That day, a true revolutionary was born, the day a great man was hanged by the British. That day has to be celebrated.'

'Then next year, we'll do it, comrade. We'll shout *lal salaam* as well.'

The humour doesn't go down well. He is offended. He takes the remains of the cake, drops it into the bin and goes to bed.

My birthday is just like any regular day. I stay at home. I make breakfast, lunch, dinner. I do the dishes. I sweep the floors. I fold clothes. I make coffee in the morning, tea in the evening. At night, I make the bed. We have sex before falling asleep. The only human interaction I have all day is with my husband.

The red dot remains stationary.

* *

three four
sweep the floor
three four
do the chore
three four
come here whore
The rhymes run in my head.

The rhymes help me keep count of the day's progress: morning, noon and night.

* *

The smallest thing could spark a major fight: the level of salt in the pumpkin *sambar*, the excess oil in the groundnut chutney, the green chilli in the chicken curry, the headline in the newspaper, the suspicion that I went to the shop without wearing a *dupatta*, the agenda for the day, the shopping list I have forgotten to prepare, the laundry piling up, the failure to bring back the clothes left to dry in the porch the night before, which are now rain-soaked and mud-splattered and have to be washed again, the sticky kitchen floor, the slow speed at which I clear the dishes, his shirt and trousers that I have not ironed. He can be kind, I know he can, I've seen how tender he is with the homeless boys in town, but with me I know that he will always choose to be cruel.

The red dot remembers the video games from its earlier life. Diablo. Mortal Kombat 3. It wants to fight back, draw its weapons and return fire, but somehow it always ends up shying away from fully fledged carnage.

The red dot wants to stay safe. It is content to accept what it is given and do as it is told.

* *

Note to myself
  one two
  get a clue

three four
say no more
five six
take the risk
seven eight
try to fight
nine ten
a free woman

* *

My husband decides to set me free. Free of my past. Free of the burden of memory. Free of the burden of lost dreams. In setting me free, he says, he is setting himself free.

He deletes the 25,600-odd emails from my Gmail inbox. All at one go. Then, to prevent me from writing to the Gmail help team and having my emails restored, he changes the password to something I do not know and cannot guess. He erases everything on my hard disk.

Everything about my life as a writer is gone. There are no contacts. There is no email conversation that I can return to at a later date. There is no past. There are no drafts of poems I sent to friends. There are no love letters. There is no history of the emails my mother sent me, typing with one finger, telling me to stay warm in Shimla when I was there for a research seminar, telling me to call home often, telling me to be happy. There is no past. I am rendered a blank slate. My husband's liberation comes from what he calls 'annihilating all material basis of your engagement with the past'.

The red dot now grows exponentially. This is the cultural revolution for a computer age. The red dot is now a red flag.

* *

Everyone at school had a hobby: they collected stamps, coins, baggage tags, train tickets, keychains, empty bottles, fridge magnets, or transfer tattoos that came with bubblegum packets. For a brief period, my hobby involved cutting out Heathcliff comic strips from *Young World* and pasting them into a fat notebook. The three minutes of precision cutting and sloppy pasting were followed by half an hour of liberally applying Fevicol on my palm, letting it dry and then peeling off glue that now looked like layers of skin. My father never noticed. My mother called it childish, but she was happy I kept myself busy with a cartoon of a misbehaving cat.

Now, as a bored housewife, who cannot even carry on the pretence of being a writer, I return to the restlessness of my childhood summers.

I make up my own hobbies. They are all the lives I could be leading in a parallel universe.

Post-doctoral fellow:
A socio-linguistic study of a dysfunctional marriage

Friday film critic:
Short synopses of movies inspired by violent husbands

Kindergarten teacher:
Teaching how to count with the help of rhymes

Games developer:
Choose-the-ending virtual reality games to simulate marriage

Anthropologist meets Agony Aunt meets
The-Everything-Expert:
Tracing the culture-specific evolutionary origins of everyday aggressions

Hobby-maker:
Suggesting hobbies for lonely, married women to keep themselves busy

These games make me feel creative and resourceful. This could be the seed of a start-up. Or a salaried position: Artist-in-Forced-Residence.

The red dot on the screen remains stationary.

* *

The biggest insult that can come a woman's way from a left-winger husband are the dreaded words: 'You are not fit for me to call you a comrade.' This is when the red dot pales into insignificance, when it becomes so minuscule that it requires a microscope to be seen.

It is an abject declaration of failure, but when my husband says these words, I hear them as a revelation. 'Comrade' and 'human' are interchangeable in his lexicon, so perhaps if I were fit to be called a comrade then he would begin treating me as a human? I spend several weeks setting about becoming the most credible, the most self-effacing, self-righteous, self-reflexive comrade that has ever worn a beret.

I learn to criticize myself for who I am. I criticize myself for my reluctance about housework. I criticize myself for my choice of clothing. I try to point out the feudal remnants in my behaviour. I take blame for the petit-bourgeois mentality that I harbour. I concede that my feminism, with its obsession about sexuality, is a middle-class project that forgets the lived realities of millions of working-class women. In the same breath I also say that I continue to think that working-class women also have sexual desires and need equal rights, and that they need feminism too. When this is met with disdain and disapproval, I talk about why such a vacillation is a hallmark of the petit-bourgeois mind, and I promise to work on it by declassing myself. I explain why I have not yet read Mao on the eight kinds of writing. I do my best to criticize myself viciously until I become a 'true comrade'.

It feels like confession. It feels like what I imagine Sunday morning confession feels like to church-goers. It feels as if

Communism was a religion, even if it swears that it is against religion.

The red dot decides to equip itself with more knowledge. Reading is the way towards a revolutionary consciousness. The red dot tries to educate itself. It connects to the internet in the half an hour it is allowed access. It looks up information. It hopes to grow from strength to strength, until it is an enormous fiery red ball, like the sun itself. Sometimes, the information confounds the red dot.

Criticism is a part of the Marxist dialectical method; as such, Communists must not fear it, but engage in it openly. (*The members of Italian flagellant confraternities were deeply involved in promoting peace. They travelled from town to town, publicly flagellating themselves.*)

Criticism may take place along comradely lines, while at the same time a basic unity is felt and preserved. This is the dialectical method. (*Their activity was invested with a variety of goals: as penance for and purgation from personal sin, as a sharing in the sufferings of Christ, a demonstration of love for and solidarity with Christ, and as expiation for the sins of humanity.*)

The red dot blinks furiously. The blinking causes the system to hang.

* *

The red dot plays anthropologist in the marriage. Its method: participant-observation. It is a bit of both: participant and observer.

The hallmark of an anthropologist is the willingness to try. (That's from Valentine. No, not the saint, a different Valentine.)

So it tries, and tries hard to familiarize itself with the field.

The act of making the strange familiar always makes the familiar a little bit strange. (That's from Wagner. No, not the composer.)

And the more familiar the strange becomes, the more and more strange the familiar appears. That's how the once-upon-a-time fiery feminist becomes a battered wife. By observing, but not doing anything. By experiencing, but not understanding. By recording but not judging.

By getting used. By no longer being the outsider. By becoming the native informant. By becoming the specimen in a lab, by becoming the case study.

The red dot needs to be saved from itself.

* *

Today, still smarting from its emptied inbox, the red dot prowls the internet looking for information about the destruction of material basis as a method for revolutionary transformation. It comes across an artist.

> Michael Landy made an inventory of everything he owned: every item of furniture, every book, every piece of food, every cat toy... The list took three years to complete and it contained 7,227 items. Then, with the help of a large machine and an overall-clad team of operatives, he set about destroying it all. After two weeks nothing but powder remained.

His work is called *Break Down*.
The red dot now becomes a big red bleeding heart.

* *

Although it is diminutive, the red dot jumps into major-league action soon enough. It has the secret pent-up energy of bored housewives.

The red dot remembers that ever since it started gaining the upper hand in arguments by quoting the same men as its adversary and arch-rival – Marx and Mao and other scare-crows – its intelligence has been insulted by claims that it is not dialectically right, that it lacks the capability to conduct a decent argument, that it does not accept criticism, that it is incapable of nuance, that its logic is inconsistent.

It schools itself in a treatise on how to debate. It learns the tightrope walk of dialectics. It learns to hold its own against rhetorical somersaulting. On those evenings, the red dot is a sharp round stone in a slingshot.

But the red dot also knows that what my husband needs is only a provocation. Something that sets him on fire, credible enough to incense him, harmful enough to make him rage through the evening, malleable enough for it all to become about my past rather than our present. So, packed with the awareness that Communism with this comrade is only control and punishment, the red dot must sometimes forgo its own ideals and back down. It stage-manages a fight of its own making; it creates its own confusion; it admits fault; it defuses him by giving him a chance to lecture; it props up a dummy altercation to prevent itself from becoming the whore while the husband becomes the abuser.

On those evenings, in self-defence mode, the red dot becomes a smoke bomb.

IX

Watch out for love
(unless it is true,
and every part of you says yes including the toes),
it will wrap you up like a mummy,
and your scream won't be heard
and none of your running will end.

ANNE SEXTON,
'ADMONITIONS TO A SPECIAL PERSON'

Always heed the warning.

Love will let you down.

* *

I stammer.

I stutter.

I sandbag my husband in the silences between my utterances.

With a man who has rehearsed his accusations, and your responses, and his response to your response, and so on, to the nth conceivable degree, with a man who will never hesitate to raise his hand to you if all else fails, with this man, to shout or argue is to lose.

To be unsure, however, is to take him by surprise; to take him by surprise is to have a fighting chance.

* *

This battle of the adversaries is structured like a chess game. Here, there are only two players. I'm the king, constantly under threat. I'm the king, who can move only one step at any given time. He's the drama queen. There is no move that he cannot make. The board is empty except for us. He corners me wherever I move. There is no hiding. In the end, he always corners me.

'Your violence is the violence of the Indian state,' he tells me. 'Your violence is structural. My violence is the counter-violence of the insurgents who are fighting for the rights of the people, the counter-violence of the women who blow themselves up to declare their nation's struggle for self-determination, the counter-violence of a little Kashmiri boy throwing a stone at a soldier. His act of violence is an act to oppose the violence of the Indian state. Edward Said threw stones at the Israelis. I am not ashamed of my violence. I am proud of it. I am not a liberal, or a democrat. My violence is a reaction to your violence. Your violence is your effort to emasculate me, to live the life of middle-class luxury, to go on talking about your feminism.'

I'm now the repressive apparatus of the state.

He is the guerrilla warrior.

This is his stubborn song.

This is an unequal war.

* *

If I stand up to him, if I shout back at him, he calls me mad. When I dismiss such a glib label, he says that it is the nature of mad people to claim to be sane.

I see, it is no longer fashionable to be mad. Depression is the word, isn't it? Three inches of cleavage, two books of poetry, plenty of sex and depression – that's all it takes to make a woman a famous writer. Beginning from Sylvia Plath to Kamala Das, that is the only trajectory you have all followed.

What I'm undergoing seems to me something far more colossal than a darkness in my head. 'Depression' is the label that he applies to my state of mind, my sense of life.

Depression is the disease that only middle-class women nurture and put on display to the world.

Depression, a symbol of the meaninglessness of bourgeois existence.

Depression is a career choice for you. Without that, you are nothing.

Depression: how much more individualistic can you be?

Depression, the privileged woman's sole ticket to victimhood.

Depression – like the cunning politician who killed his mother on the eve of election day – a raft on which to ride a wave of sympathy.

Sometimes, he does not theorize at all, does not diagnose my anger and develop his conjectures.

These are the things that happen when there is an insect inside your head. Mandapoochi di. It digs and crawls and squirms and gets restless and your thoughts go in all directions.

When it is not depression, when it is not this restless insect flying around in my brain and eating away all the softer parts that programme me to be an obedient wife, he blames it on the demons that have possessed me.

* *

Depression is not the only context in which he diagnoses me as being middle-class. On the rare occasion where sex leads to an involuntary moan in bed, he tells me to shut the fuck up, and he stops the act itself, as if to punish me for putting my pleasure before his. What follows is an inter-coital discourse on the class analysis of sexual behaviour. *You are making a spectacle out of love. You are screaming because this is a performance for you.*

As if to confirm his suspicions, he hits the boy who comes once a week to water the rows of leather-leafed croton plants in the garden, accusing him of voyeurism. His paranoia takes on newer forms. He obsessively fills the keyhole of the connecting rooms with chewing gum. He rolls blankets and wads them in the little space under the doors. He is soundproofing the rooms as best as he can. One day, when he finds the chewing gum gone from the keyhole, he waits for the gardener boy and lashes him mercilessly with a length of hosepipe. I try to reason with him that perhaps ants or rats might have taken the gum. He doesn't believe in any possible or passable explanation. He believes in eliminating any evidence that we have sex.

This reaches a stage where our foreplay begins on the bed, and shifts to the floor to stop the creaking of the bedstead matching the rhythm of our bodies.

Sex with this man is the death of spontaneity. Sex is the opposite of intimacy because the more he worries about the noise-question, the more he obsesses about the gardener, the less and less aware I become of pleasure itself.

* *

I make an effort to change the effects of his conditioning. I do not enter into the complicated domain of rights theory – knowing that the minute I say 'It is my right,' the idea will be shouted down before I have finished the sentence. I opt to talk to him about my sexual moaning as an inevitability, as a natural occurrence, as something that we are programmed to do as human beings. I read to him the lines from *The Vagina Monologues: I realized moans were best when they caught you by surprise, they came out of this hidden mysterious part of you that was speaking its own language. I realized that moans were, in fact, that language.* I drag the weight of my linguistics education to ram home the point. This is a function of language, I say. Roman Jakobson came up with six functions of language – I do not remember the names of each of them – but this is one of them. This is the emotive function. This is how our languages are designed, this is hardwired into us, this is how we express ourselves at our most primal level.

Hearing me, he looks lost. To understand this function of language is beyond my husband. I try listing examples that exist beyond human beings: the mad songs of cuckoos in their mating season. The soft, low notes of a lonely whale. The deathly howl of cats. He does not get it.

In his rule book – sown by patriarchy, watered by feudalism, manured by a selective interpretation of Communism – a woman should not moan. That is how history steals her voice.

* *

To cast out the demon, even the kindest Tamil witch-doctors believe that the possessed woman must be whipped. It does not matter if the woman screams, because the belief is that the demon leaves her through her mouth. Sometimes the whipping continues until she is silent and no longer able to scream. Sometimes the whipping goes on all night, until the woman collapses, unconscious. Unless the possessed woman is beaten, it is believed that the demon in her does not enter into a discussion, it does not answer questions, it evades revealing its identity. In our marriage, my husband is the witch-doctor. He wants to drive out the demons that he thinks have possessed me. In the absence of bunches of fresh neem leaves to strike me with – bitter, serrated, midnight-green – he uses makeshift substitutes: my Mac's power cord, his leather belt, twisted electrical cables. My demons are not happy. They do not want to leave me to the mercy of this man. They decide to stay.

* *

When he hits me, the most frightening part is not the pain and the possible scarring and the perverted sense of shame. It is not in knowing that I'm defeated, or in the realization that I am not physically strong enough to match him blow for blow, that I cannot teach him a lesson never to mess with me.

When he hits me, the terror follows from the instinct that this will go further, that this does not end easily, that today it is my arms that he is punching, but tomorrow it will be my hair that he will wind around his palm to drag me through the rooms, the next day it will be my backbone that will endure a shattering blow, the day after that it will be my head on which his angry fists will descend.

When he hits me, these thoughts pile on in quick succession.

When he hits me, the terror flows from the fear that today he uses his bare hands, but tomorrow he could wield a heavy-buckled belt, he could grab an iron rod, he could throw a chair, that he could break open my head against a wall.

Every day, I inch closer to death, to dying, to being killed, to the fear that I will end up in a fight whose result I cannot reverse.

I know that he knows this too.

The use of force is always to signal the impending threat of greater force. The fear that he seeks to instill in me is never the actual act itself, but the fear of where the act can lead to. What I see is what I am made to foresee.

155

When he hits me, and I do this every time he hits me, I cry aloud: 'This is the last time. Forgive me. Give me this last chance. This will never happen again.'

I think what I mean is not 'This (mistake) will never happen again' because I know my husband well enough to know that he will endlessly find mistakes in what I do. I think my desperate cry is actually the promise that I seek from him, from his cruelty and his short temper, from his violence and his chastisement, as if by saying from my lips 'This will never happen again' I expect him to echo and match that sentiment, I expect that this cessation of whatever misdemeanour on my part will be countered and compensated by a cessation of violence on his part, and whenever I cry 'This will never happen again', I'm actually declaring a ceasefire on behalf of both of us.

That is not how peace is born, I lack all experience to know this crucial fact.

* *

I tell my parents about the violence. I want to leave. I cannot take this anymore. It has only been a handful of months, but I feel defeated. They take turns convincing me to stay.

* *

My father on the phone:
What is going on? Well, that is common. It is a matter of ego.

I know you, you are my daughter, you do not like to lose a fight. The marriage is a give and take. Listen to him. He only means well. Do not raise your voice. Do not talk back. Yes, I know. It is difficult. But remember, only if you respond he is going to talk back and things escalate. Silence is a shield and it is also a weapon. Learn how to use it. Why else do we say, 'amaidhiya ponga'? Silence is peace. You cannot make peace unless you hold your tongue. Yes. Anyway, don't trouble your mother about this. It will upset her for no reason. Take care.

* *

My father on the phone:
Yes, I know, I know. I told her you called. I said you wanted to talk to her. I have no reason to lie to you, dear. No, I am not protecting her. Is that what you think of me? You do not live here anymore so you have forgotten how busy it gets. There is not even five minutes to spare. We have not had any time to even talk to each other. You take care. Be a smart girl. There is someone at the door. I am going now.

* *

My mother on the phone:
Why, dear, why? It hasn't been long at all. The first year is the worst year. Tell me about it. It is maddening, it will drive you to suicide. You will be wondering what you are doing with

157

him. I survived it. It was not easy, but over time you forget all the sadness.

* *

My father on the phone:
Is that what he actually said? Rascal. Is this what his Communism has come to? You should cut off his balls and send them back to where he came from. It is becoming impossible to find good young men. Maybe after you both move back to Chennai, we will be in a position to help. I don't know what he does, but perhaps, this is how he spends his time all day, planning what he is going to fight with you about? Keep him occupied. Okay, don't worry I will ask your mother to call you back. You take care.

* *

My mother on the phone:
All change is slow. A marriage is not magic.
    You will have to give him time. He will come around.

* *

My father on the phone:
Yes. Yes. That is not very nice. Listen. Patience. Patience. *Porumai.* Tolerance. Just tolerate. *Sahippu thanmai.* This is not a time to be selfish. If you break off your marriage, everyone in town will mock me. They will say his daughter ran

away in less than six months. It will reflect on your upbringing. This is not what I intended for my daughter. You have no idea what a father goes through. A father of a daughter – that is a special kind of punishment. We pay the price. Please. Think about us this once.

* *

My mother on the phone:
So you want to be like all these writers you read about and those writers whom you call your friends – single and sleeping around with anyone they please. That happens only in stories. I have friends who tried to be like that. Not writers, just women. They died very sad deaths. They died alone.

* *

My father on the phone:
What now? Listen to me. I am an old man. I have seen many people, many marriages. These problems arise, these problems disappear. These problems will cease to exist when you have children. Do not talk too much. Never in history has anything been solved by constantly talking. Good character resides only where anger resides. These two are inseparable. His anger and rage are misdirected. He means well. Do not drag these problems home to us, do not let these wounds fester. Learn to obey. You can question his decisions later. I have said this to you a million times.

* *

My mother on the phone:
What can I say? I can suggest you leave him, start again. How long would that cycle go on? What if you fail again, with another man? What is the guarantee that he will not be another monster? Finding the perfect man is a myth. Do not believe in it, work with what you have.

* *

My father on the phone:
He is hitting you? The bastard. Ah, my daughter. I would have imagined you hitting him. Just try to avoid conflict as much as possible. What can we do? We could talk to him and take your side but he will assume the whole family is against him. That will turn him against you even more. You are alone as it is. Yeah. So, if we talk to him about this, we will have to be on his side de facto, but that will make him feel vindicated, and he will crush you all the more. Our interfering will not benefit you anyway. But remember, we are with you. Clench your teeth and wait it out. Take care of yourself, take care of him. Tell him that I sent him my regards.

* *

I listen to my father's advice:
'Hold your tongue. He is your husband, not your enemy.'

'Do not talk back. You can never take back what you have said.'

'Your word-wounds will never heal, they will remain long after both of you have patched up and made peace.'

'It takes two to fight. He cannot fight by himself. It will drain his energy, to fight alone.'

'Do not talk too much. Never in history has anything been solved by constantly talking.'

'Don't you understand? Silence is golden.'

I climb into the incredible sadness of silence. Wrap its slowness around my shoulders, conceal its shame within the folds of my sari. Make it a vow, as if my life hinged upon it, as if I was not a wife in Mangalore but a nun elsewhere, cloistered and clinging to her silence to make sense of the world.

To stay silent is to censor all conversation. To stay silent is to erase individuality. To stay silent is an act of self-flagellation because this is when the words visit me, flooding me with their presence, kissing my lips, refusing to dislodge themselves from my tongue.

I do not allow myself anything more than the essential necessities of domestic existence. The questions about what my husband wants to eat, when he wants to be woken up, whether the electricity bill has been paid. The minimal interaction bestows an almost formal character to our marriage. He cannot step across that line.

I am unfazed when he assumes that this silence stems

from my defeat. He sees it as a sign of victory. He praises me for realizing my folly, for listening to him, for finally coming to my senses. I do not dispute his claim. I do not accept it either. I simply stare at him with vacant eyes, give him a vacant nod.

It irritates him that he cannot walk away with the trophy of victory. He brushes off my wordlessness as childish, and maintains that, sooner rather than later, I will have to reform myself and repent my mistakes. He cannot push me any further than this, and so, he retreats.

My silence settles on us like incessant rain. It stills the humdrum of the everyday. It leaves us stranded in our own little puddles.

I enjoy this brief interlude. My silence becomes an invincible shield. He attempts to penetrate its surface with every conceivable tactic to provoke me into conversation, but he fails. He is left listening to his own words, building his own arguments, eating his own anger.

He reads this as rejection. He is quick to turn the tables on me. He accuses me of inhabiting a world in my mind, a world where I am cohabiting with ex-lovers, a world where I have left him. He asks me to stop leading a double life, tells me that if I believe that I am Andal, living with some imaginary Thirumaal, I have no place in his home. He offers to check me into a mental hospital.

I am unwilling to address his accusations, unwilling to face the consequences of an unwise retort. I do not say anything in my defence. To talk to him, as he is raging against me, would only feed his fury. He is in no mood to listen in any case.

He kicks me in the stomach. 'Prove it!' he yells as I double over. 'Prove it to me that you are my wife. Prove it to me that you are not thinking of another man. Or I will prove it for you.'

My hair is gathered up in a bunch in his hand now. He is lifting me by my hair alone. All the blood is rushing to my head, my thighs fight to feel the hard wood of the chair. I am in pain. He drags me from the table and into the bedroom. I feel the heavy, funereal drumbeats of marriage as he forces my sari up around my waist. They grow louder and faster, restless in their hurry to drown out everything else. I close my eyes now, afraid, the way I did during the wedding ceremony, when rice was flung at us and prayers were chanted. The fire that made our union sacred and eternal now blazes in the parting of my thighs.

There are no moans, only screams. Screams precede my speech. Screams help me transition from silence to begging him to stop. His reply is like water bursting a dam. 'Why do you talk to me now? Why? How did you find all your words all of a sudden? So, this is the miracle cure to your silence, is it? If you wanted to be fucked like a bitch, you could have asked me. See, you have got your speech back. See, you have been cured. Now keep your mouth shut and don't wake the neighbours. You are a whore. *Thevidiya*. You should know that. Stop crying, there is nothing to cry about. I should be crying for marrying a whore. You are a whore. This is what whores do. This is why I don't treat you like a wife. Stay still. You don't want it this way? How many men took you from behind? How many? Would you even remember? Don't fight or this is going to hurt you. Fucking cheap whore. Next time you taunt me with your silence I will tear your fucking cunt apart. Now say sorry, bitch. Say sorry. Yes. That's it. You will remember this. You will never forget this lesson.'

X

Whore, he spits, at she who keeps
thousands of her lovers hidden.
Inside the pillow covers,
the bedspread, the rolled-up mat,
the bookshelf, the attic or the spice box?
His previous lovers
never caused such betrayal.
Nights thicken into a coir-rope
spun out of reproaches.

All his fear:
Will she just knead the dust
to bake a man? That too, with a penis
as large as an elephant's trunk?

MALATHI MAITHRI,
'THE THOUSAND AND SECOND NIGHT'

I never understood rape until it happened to me. It was a concept – of savagery, of violence, of violation, of disrespect. I had read my share of Kate Millett and Susan Brownmiller but nothing prepared me for how to handle it. Within a marriage, fighting back comes with its consequences. The man who rapes me is not a stranger who runs away. He is not the silhouette in the car park, he is not the masked assaulter, he is not the acquaintance who has spiked my drinks. He is someone who wakes up next to me. He is the husband for whom I have to make coffee the following morning. He is the husband who can shrug it away and tell me to stop imagining things. He is the husband who can blame his actions on unbridled passion the next day, while I hobble from room to room.

I begin to learn that there are no screams that are loud enough to make a husband stop. There are no screams that cannot be silenced by the shock of a tight slap. There is no organic defence that can protect against penetration. He covers himself with enough lubricant to slide past all my resistance. My legs go limp. I come apart.

* *

How do I explain to anyone this savage rite? Where do I look for metaphors? How do I let another person know how it feels to be raped within a marriage? Death is all that I can think about when I lie there. Death which brings with it many meaningless rituals. To the Tamils, the most important ritual is the ceremonial feeding of the corpse. Before the body is hauled to the cremation ground, before the distant mourners start arriving and weeping, before drunken drums take to the streets, next of kin place grains of uncooked rice in the mouth of the dead body. Motionless, devoid of touch taste sight smell sound, the corpse feels nothing. It lies there, playing the role of the obedient half of an obligatory ritual, as close relatives drop white rice through its parted lips. It is a feeling of unfeeling. It is how I feel when my husband's kisses fall into my mouth as he parts my legs and begins pushing.

* *

Sex, actually rape, becomes his weapon to tame me. Your cunt will be ruined, he tells me. Your cunt will turn so wasted, so useless you will never be able to offer yourself to any man. It'll be as wide as a begging bowl. *Koodhi kizhinja, paati surukku pai pola iruppadi.*

I imagine my vagina falling out of me like spare change. Not with jingling noises, but in a wet, pulpy, silent way, carrying the purple of dying roses.

When he takes me, I dream of how I'm going to lose this part of me.

Perhaps it'll come away in slabs of blood and pink flesh. It may not go alone, bringing my uterus and ovaries out with it. On a toilet seat someday, I will notice that I'm passing my pleasure. A slow death by disintegration.

The fear makes me withdraw into myself. The terror seizes me like a spirit the minute my legs are spread.

* *

As much as it resists rape, my body has also learnt how to surrender. It learns to shut its eyes, it learns to look away. It knows to kneel on all fours and await its own humiliation. It learns to play dead. It learns to wait. It learns to extend its own threshold of pain and shame and brutality. And yet, there is no such thing as preemptive sex. There is no way in which I can make an offering of voluntary sex to prevent myself from getting raped afterwards. It does not work like that. If there was, then I would have avoided many nights of rape.

* *

The shame of rape is the shame of the unspeakable. Women have found it easier to jump into fire, consume poison, blow themselves up as suicide bombers, than tell another soul about what happened. A rape is a fight you did not win. You could not win.

A rape is defeat.

* *

A rape is also punishment. Sometimes, the punishment for saying no. Sometimes, the punishment for a long-ago love story.

In Tamil culture, menstruation pollutes the body for a period of three days. After childbirth, the body remains polluted for eleven days; and for the death of a blood relative, we are considered soiled for sixteen days. For sex with another man before marriage, a husband considers his wife polluted for a lifetime. A body that is considered polluted can be punished as a man pleases. That is the philosophy of caste, that is the philosophy of my rape.

* *

How? is eight times more popular than its nearest interrogative rival, *Who?*

Where? When? Why? What? They come far, far behind on that list. Google will tell you this, when we, the people, ask about the questions that we, the people, ask.

My husband is like other people, his endless question-on-a-loop begins with *How?* But, my husband is also a unique individual, so he brings in his own addition.

He asks me, not *How?*, but *How many?*

As in: *How many men have fucked you?*

In his defence it could be argued that he simply likes to pay attention to detail.

* *

The coarseness of my husband's insults makes me cringe. I'm ashamed that language allows a man to insult a woman in an infinite number of ways. Every image conjured up is repellent. Every part of my body is a word spat out in disgust. My cunt, sequestered and quarantined, is nothing but a spittoon for his insults.

Once, this language was something else for me. It was a secret place of pleasure. It was my face in the water, the sudden comfort of far-away laughter, the smell of woodsmoke clinging to my hair, the eager arrival of my breasts – it was all mine to explore. Like a lover's body, there were things about my language that I thought only I knew.

I remember mining my language for words from the deepest, most forgotten seams, words that people no longer wrap around their tongues, words that stay mouldering in lexicons and old works of literature that nobody bothers to read anymore. I found the word for a flirtatious girl who chatters too much, the word for the first meeting of the eyes of two people who will eventually fall in love, the word for an intoxicating drink that induces dance. Keep in mind that this is a language where the word for obstinacy is also the word for intercourse.

Slut is not only a woman who wants sex, as in English. In this part of India, it is the dirty woman, but also the disrespectful one, the fight-loving woman, the quarrel-monger.

In Tamil, I discovered words to describe the delirious fever from aggressive sex and the deep sleep that immediately descends on satisfied lovers. One word, for the practice of having sex with a woman selected by a drawing of lots on a festive day, confirmed my worst suspicions about my culture.

Sex, as a sensory experience, lurks around other corners: there is a readymade word for the pervading smell that follows an act of coitus, another for the paleness that settles on a woman's sad skin when her lover is long gone. My curiosity kept me engaged, kept me going back.

In the completely refined and absolutely unused formal version of my language, the word for blow job can also be loosely translated as a face-ride. In the same sanitized dictionary of this agglutinative tongue, the clitoris is, among other names, a compound word – *yonilingam* – the vagina penis. I joked about this juxtaposition with my politician-lover. He corrected me, wrote back to gently chide me that I should know better, this word is never on anyone's lips, and introduced a word from the soft porn of his student days: *mathanapeetam*. The highest seat of lovemaking, the headquarters if you like.

Every once in a while I allowed my politician-lover to enter my translator's territory. I gave him the unadulterated pleasure of etymology. *Mulaikann*. Eye of the breast. Areola. *Mulaikaambu*. Stalk of the breast. Nipple. And then again: *mulai*. Breast. Also meaning, as a verb, sprout. He would whisper the names to the parts of my body, using the rough words of the street, employing the same deliberate slowness as when he used the words of poets. I learnt from him a word for the wetness that wells up between a woman's legs. I had never encountered that word before. This is one of those words that only travel within a language from lover to lover. Years later, I realized that though these words move in this slow, nomadic way, everyone, eventually, learns them.

* *

I try to reconcile the world that I witness with the linguistic theory that I have learnt.

Here, the inversion of Luce Irigaray. Not: *Ta langue, dans ma bouche, m'a-t-elle obligée à parler?* Not: Was it your tongue in my mouth that forced me into speech?

No, Lucy. Not speech, but silence.

Within my marriage, I have the conclusive results of scientific method: it was your tongue in your mouth that forced me into silence. It was your tongue in your mouth that forced me into submission. And then, it was your tongue in my mouth that forced me.

* *

As rapes become a regular occurrence, I reach the point of no return. I play rag-doll and normalize it; I learn to normalize the violence in his words. His insults degrade me, as if through the act of calling me whore and slut and every conceivable swear-word, my body becomes a necessary receptacle to this rape. Good women don't have bad things happen to them – in order to be raped, I need first to be made into this caricature of a bad woman. This male psychosexual logic looks at penetration as punishment. This is the rape that disciplines, the rape that penalizes me for the life I have presumably led. This is the rape that tames, the rape that puts me on the path of being a good wife. This is the rape whose aim is to inspire regret in me. This is the rape whose aim is to make me understand that my husband can do with my body as he pleases. This is rape as ownership. This rape contains a husband's rage against all the men who may have touched me, against all the men who may touch me, against all the men who may have desired me. This nightly rape comes with a one-point agenda: she must derive no pleasure from sex. And yet, whenever he takes me against my will, he taunts me for enjoying it. In his ironclad logic: I am a whore, so I can be raped; I let myself be raped, so I am a whore.

* *

Popular opinion suggests that the greatest Indian film ever made – a 'curry western' in Western academic classification – was *Sholay*. Unable to come to terms with the idea that I might end up being disappointed with the best of Bollywood, I never watched it. But, like everyone who only reads about movies in newspapers, and never goes to cinemas or turns on the television, I know its most important line of dialogue.

Kitne aadmi thay?

How many men were there?

I do not know what comes before that line. I do not know what comes after. I do not know the context, except perhaps that the villain wants to know, and he is angry, and he is quite demanding. I hear this question again and again. In rough Tamil. Often, in bed, as he penetrates me.

When I hear my husband ask me *howmanymen*, I do not answer. I have not watched *Sholay*. I do not know what is the answer. I lie there dreaming of rocky hilltops and songs and dances and murders and gunshots.

* *

In a life I led long before I was married, I'm the poet who wrote: *After the fifth man, every woman becomes a temple.*

* *

'Why are you so fascinated by other men?' I ask in a low voice as we tour the marketplace together, picking out okra for dinner and giving tight smiles to the other shoppers. There are hundreds of people around us. It is the only reason I have the courage to ask him.

'It's you who are fascinated,' he hisses back. 'You dream of the day when you will carry your cunt into another man's bed. Well, don't. When I'm through, what you have will be torn and tattered. After a child, it will not even be recognizable.'

That is the aim of his rapes, all this rough sex. Not just a disciplining, but a disabling. He believes that after him, I will have nothing left in me to love, to make love, to give pleasure.

This is a man breaking his own wife. This is a man burning down his own house.

XI

At the end of the day, we can endure much more than we think we can.

FRIDA KAHLO

'Will you walk out of this marriage?'

It's a question I never answer one way or another. I answer him with other questions, or with a declaration of everlasting love.

There's no honest answer. Only answers that make my life safer, the nights less painful.

The brave die every day because they do not back down.

* *

What happens to those not brave enough, I wonder? And what happens to those who are too brave for their own good?

Every day, newspapers smelling of fresh kill bring us morbidity from Central India. Defiant tribal women raped, mutilated and dressed up in combat gear for the photographs. Portrayed as Maoists because body counts help paramilitary forces. Their stark-naked corpses returned to their parents wrapped in clear plastic. Prisons filled to thrice the maximum capacity with young, idealistic men. The horrors of third-degree torture visited upon those who preach a different politics – tortures without traces. A long splinter from a coconut broom, doused in petrol, forced up the penis, followed by holding a lighter aflame at its orifice. An internal burn that no medical examination would red-flag. The unbearable, endless enumeration of these atrocities each passing day.

I wish I was just a writer taking in the tragedy.

I'm not. I'm wife. I watch my husband become unhinged and destabilized by the daily flow of reports. Afraid that the hunt will one day come to our doorstep, he begins to take a perverse pleasure in narrating and boasting of his guerrilla days.

'I've smuggled AK47s. We ripped apart a Tata Safari and had the weapons fitted into the metal frame of the seats. I brought it along from Chhattisgarh to Chennai, right under the nose of the great Indian police.

'I once ran a typing institute in the south. Decoy operation, I had to provide a cover for a senior leader who was undergoing treatment.

'Had to kill a soldier once. He had fucked a girl against her will and was now torturing her little sister who he snatched from the road to school. The instruction was to throw him over the bridge. You want to know what I did? I disembowelled him. Not one man in his platoon would have the guts to be inappropriate to women after they saw his corpse. Even the party was angry that I went beyond my brief.

'They had me sent to Bhutan to hide, afraid the forces would come after me. I became Thinley Dorji. I was to keep a low profile. Low profile doesn't exist in my dictionary. In three months, I had perfected a plot to assassinate the king. They called me back to avoid trouble.'

The isolation of our marriage feeds his words. He speaks of his exploits unceasingly and in the most graphic language possible. I cannot rule out if all this is an experiment to control me. Having got used to the nightly bedroom violence, I have become less afraid and so the more menacing his story-telling grows. I can no longer sift fact from fiction.

* *

'Will you walk out of this marriage?'

The old, familiar question after many days. He is sitting at the kitchen table, crossing and uncrossing his legs nervously. I refuse to answer him, instead I challenge him with a blank stare. He laughs aloud to dismiss his own anxiety.

He does not wait for my answer. He provides it.

'Nobody is going to save you. The men who are out there, waiting for you to walk out, are waiting for their turn to ride you. The women cheering you to leave me have two intentions – they want to see you ruined, lonely, miserable. Or, they want a drama absent in their own lives. If you're banking on these men or women to fix up your life, you are making a mistake.

'Your fellow feminists, middle-class petit-bourgeois women, have found the "freedom" they need by getting rid of their man and are free to fuck around.

'Now go, make yourself useful. I'm hungry.'

* *

What makes a woman stay in a marriage that she should have left the day before it even happened? The need to prove a point – to those who publicly bet that a woman writer like her cannot stay married for more than four weeks, to those who bet that she was incapable of commitment, to her mother who told her to wait till she was older to settle down. To add to the list there is fear; the pressure of family; and, also, hope.

Hope prevents me from taking my own life. Hope is the kind voice in my head that prevents me from fleeing. Hope is the traitor that chains me to this marriage.

The hope that things will change for the better tomorrow. The hope that he will eventually give up violence. Hope – as the cliché goes – is the last thing to disappear. I sometimes wish it had abandoned me first, with no farewell note or goodbye hug, and forced me to act.

* *

How could I rely on anyone to intervene?

I consider going to the police, but when I contemplate it in the solitude of lonely afternoons, I understand that it is impossible. If he caught scent of my plans, I know how he would react. He would surrender as a former Maoist fighter, claim the offered amnesty and rehabilitation money, and, in exchange for a new job and police protection, betray his comrades. He would probably want his revenge on me as well, so he would denounce me as a political courier, implicating me as a terrorist. Given a choice between punishing a wife-beating rapist, and having an opportunity to milk an ex-guerrilla for intelligence, I know where the interests of the state machinery would be.

For the sake of self-preservation, I know that the police route – the first port of call for any abused woman – is closed to me.

Family and friends are my only option. But he plays the role of dutiful son-in-law to my parents. He weeps over the phone to my father. He begs my mother to tell me to be more obedient. He tells his relatives that I do not feed him properly. He hints to the only neighbours around that I'm anti-social, that I'm one of the intellectual types who prefers her own company. The bigger the circle of spectators, the more nuanced his portrait of me becomes and the less inclined people are to believe that there is no substance to his lies. To women, he evokes sympathy by saying that I constantly compare him to other men. To men, he peddles the story that I'm jealous, that I do not tolerate his female students.

I'm the battered woman, but he is the one who is playing the role of the victim.

My escape cannot come through these people. He is too effective at giving his version of events; too quick to ask grovellingly for their advice; too good at flattering them with his attentions. He pushes my friends and family into the territory of the neutral; he asks them to play fair. No one wants to give a guilty verdict to the man who is prepared to elevate them to the role of judge and jury.

* *

Every arbitration seems to end in his favour, yet it still does not placate him. He knows I am not bound to anyone else's words or appeals. When arguments between us cannot be resolved by outside intervention, he resorts to threats. He instills a raw bleeding fear in me in the belief that I will be too afraid to act.

'I will skin your scalp. It will be slow, but I will do a very thorough job of it. It will be very painful, but precision always has its element of pain. All this beauty that you boast about will be gone. Your hair will be gone. I will be kind. I will remove every mirror from your presence. This punishment is not only for you. You will not die. Not immediately anyway. I will call your father to come and collect you. You will stay alive long enough for him to reach here and see you in this state. And he will know then what happens when he brings up a whore. This is a price he has to pay. I will be long gone by then. You cannot find me. Your father cannot find me. You may go to the police, but wait, you will need to go to a hospital first. Or to the burial ground. And if the police come, even if they begin to hunt for me, they will never find me. I will go underground. I will be a different man with a new name and speaking another language. Even you will not be able to recognize me. The police cannot do anything. I know how to slip out of their hands. I've done it many times before.'

It is incredible, his monologue. In his words, I find the feverish mirror image of his enemy: the state machinery chopping off breasts of female fighters, splashing captured militants with acid, yanking away their limbs to let them bleed to death, dancing with its military boots on the faces of slain guerrillas to render them beyond recognition. I search his eyes for just a glimpse that he recognizes how absurd he sounds, how inhuman he has himself become, but the hollow look he returns is of something that has become extinct.

* *

I have watched him play all the roles. The doting husband in the presence of his colleagues, the harassed victim of a suspicious wife to his male friends, the unjustly emasculated man to my female friends, the pleading son-in-law to my parents. The role of would-be-murderer, however, is new. I try to forget the haunting image of the white of my skull. Instead, I retreat to the comfort of the cinematic imagination. The scene forms itself. I'm lying dead in a room, looking at my corpse from outside a window. It has no hair, of course, but also no eyes. It has no mouth. It has achieved the blankness that I never managed to achieve in life. The rain lashes around and through my ghost. I picture my husband in the white clothing of a sad widower. He is sitting cross-legged on the floor. I see him with his head shorn of all hair, wearing his symbolism of heartbreak as evidence of his love. I hear him weep the most moving lament. I see him beat his head and chest. He looks broken. Between my fresh corpse and his exaggerated sorrow, my ghost-heart breaks for him. The image of my death makes him appear as the one who has lost something, not the other way around. I walk away from the window with very hesitant steps, leaving my corpse there with him. I'm on the highway. The scene dissolves with a rain-drenched shot of a city that is a stranger to me.

When I cut back to reality, there's a part of me that scoffs at the possibility of him going so far as to kill me. Then again, four months ago, I would have scoffed at the idea of being beaten by a man, or being raped by my husband. I put myself back on screen. This time I'm sitting in Morgan Freeman's white God chair, swivelling around and smoking a cigarette. I hear myself speak in the voice of God. *You are more useful alive than dead. You are more useful alive than dead. You are more useful alive than dead.*

I do not want to do anything that would endanger my life. I do not want to do anything that would allow my killer to pretend to be the bereaved husband enveloped in an aura of tragedy. So, I stay quiet and do as I'm told.

* *

In the beginning, only widows were burnt to death: tied to their dead man's pyre and set alight. That was because they wanted to get rid of the surplus women in society, they wanted to preserve the caste order. And then, when we got rid of one evil, another started to take its place. In the greedy quest for more and more dowry, or because women did not give birth to sons, or because they refused to sleep with their husbands every night, our culture started burning brides.

Tradition never goes out of fashion. Remaining in public memory, it wears new clothes. In India, a bride is burnt every ninety minutes. The time it takes to fix a quick dinner. The time it takes to do the dishes. The time it takes to wash a load of clothing. The time it takes to commute to work. This is the official statistic – the deaths the police do not even bother trying to hide in semantics. The real truth lies in the wailing that never ceases at the burns wards of hospitals.

Stuck here alone, I count the passage of hours by the number of brides who have been burnt to death. At least a hundred women reduced to their charred remains every week. Their murders written away as suicides or mishaps, a test of fire where no wife returns alive.

Fire has been established as the easiest way to kill an unnecessary wife. Knives, poisoning, hanging – the needle of suspicion in other methods of murder would point to the husband. Fire can be faked, however, made to look like a real accident. The fear of being burnt to death seizes me. Fear takes me to strange places. It paralyses me. Even in the middle of a downpour, I leave the windows open before I switch on the gas stove. I light matchsticks in the empty air before I open the valve of the gas cylinder. I step into my kitchen like someone steps into a land filled with Claymore mines.

Marriage has made sure that this is the space where I spend most of my living day. I do not want my kitchen to become my funeral pyre.

* *

My fears multiply like rats in monsoon season. Getting restless at night, their constant, scurrying feet prevent me from falling asleep. As I lie next to my husband, I'm aware of their presence all the time. Something gnaws at my fingers and nips at my toes. Something that eludes being captured or sighted. I try to trace them, lay little traps for them where I can, find out how many of them exist. Most of them have come from my husband, because he has himself made these threats, never mincing his words. Others come from what I have read in the papers, seen on television serials, heard in general gossip-at-large, the word on the street. The ability to pin them down and list them out sets me at peace. As if the information would empower me, as if knowing more would banish all the fears.

What haunts me most now was a story that at first had me laughing. During a semester when I learnt about French philosophers, the six of us who had chosen the elective prevented our degeneration into abstraction by digging up all the dirt we could find on everyone in our reading list. We were outraged that Simone de Beauvoir had passed on her young lovers to Sartre; sad that the world had lost Foucault to AIDS; engrossed with the entire Spivak–Kristeva female rivalry. That no one in the city, outside of the half a dozen of us, cared about these stories only encouraged us. That is where I first heard the story that holds me hostage today. First, it started as a joke – Althusser learnt to masturbate only in his twenties; intellectually overdeveloped, sexually underdeveloped. But then Althusser wasn't a laughing matter anymore, because one day I discovered that he had strangled his wife to death.

Later, in his memoirs, he would write about this. In slow, meandering prose he would describe how *he was massaging her neck*, how *he pressed his thumbs into the hollow at the top of her breastbone*, how *he moved them both, one to the left, one to the right up towards her ears where the flesh was hard*, how *the muscles in his forearms began to feel very tired*, how **he* was terror-struck that *her* eyes stared interminably*. He would later argue that this was how his wife would have wanted it. He would rationalize it with his theory as suicide-by-proxy. A kind of non-consensual consent. A *no* meaning a *yes*. She *wanted* it. His followers would advance the argument that her body did not show any evidence of struggle. Because he was an intellectual, he had the guile to legitimize the murder. Because he was an influential professor, he could make others stand in his support. Because he had an anti-establishment reputation, even the state absolved him.

Althusser's wife: her name was Hélène. I remember that clearly. She was killed, she could not tell her story. He had lived long enough afterward not only to tell his story, but also to cast himself as the victim. I am afraid of becoming her.

This fear is the permanent attic-rat-in-residence. This is the fear that does not go away.

* *

There is the fear of death and dying and being killed. Then, there is the other fear. The life sentence in lieu of the death warrant. The fear that I grow afraid of naming, that is wrapped tight around me like skin on a garlic pod, that restricts my breathing, that I sidestep instead of confronting: the fear of giving birth.

This marriage, oppressive and impossible as it is, does not have the power to hold me hostage forever. But, if I were to be burdened with a child, I do not know how I could walk away. I anticipate my parents forcing me to stay with him for the sake of society, I anticipate society asking me to stay with him for the sake of the child, I anticipate my own child asking

190

me to stay with him for the sake of family reputation. I cannot have that happening.

In Tamil, there is a beautiful word for the womb. *Karu-varai*. The room of the foetus. *Karuvarai*. It is what the inner sanctum of a temple is called, where a god or a goddess resides. It is a place of peace. To keep it empty is what I have decided to do. My husband has other ideas.

XII

She knew now that marriage did not make love. Janie's first dream was dead, so she became a woman.

ZORA NEALE HURSTON,
THEIR EYES WERE WATCHING GOD

Four months into marriage, polite enquiries about providing 'good news' have already turned into a pressing demand to produce a child. My husband is the only male heir for his grandparents on both sides, and this fact blossoms into questions on the future of this family tree. For reasons beyond posterity, my husband has also become convinced that what is lacking in our marriage is a child. He sees it as a measure that will fix our relationship and bind us together.

A visit to the gynaecologist is the first step. But I do not want the child of a man who beats me. I do not want to carry a child and bring it into a world because I was raped within a marriage, on a bed where my 'no' held no meaning. I'm distraught. I fight to stay back at home. He throws things around the house. He leaves a ladle on the gas stove, threatens to burn himself if I do not go with him. I will him to do it; I want him to hurt. I refuse to leave the house. Calmly, he removes the red-hot ladle from the stove and pushes it into the flesh of his left calf, right above the ankle. I miss the hiss of scorching skin because I begin to scream. I disarm him. I pull him away. He is insistent that we leave immediately, that we do not miss the appointment. He doesn't even stop to attend to the dark shape of the burn. I follow him mutely into an auto-rickshaw.

It's a dark night, there are dim lights on the street, the

rain is a shroud on the city. The auto-driver is a silhouette against the road. My husband, tall and imposing, is another silhouette. His form fills the entire space of the auto, but he somehow feels absent; his face impassive in the shadows. The city passes through me as we drive. In that darkness, his phone rings. He answers it and greets a man from his village. They talk, they talk about me, and then he holds the phone out to me. 'My vagrant cousin, he wants to say hello.'

'Hello? Hello?' Then, a low voice, abrupt and direct, whispers into the shell of my ear: 'Your husband acts like Mister Righteous. He is a fraud. The biggest fraud in our village. He was married before he married you.' I am stunned. The words loop through my head: 'He was married before he married you.' I don't know how to respond, but the next second, the cousin slides back into everyday prattle. 'What did you make for lunch today? You must come to the village sometime. I have only seen you in the photographs, this is the first time I'm talking to you, this makes me very happy. You take care of my cousin brother.' In a daze, I continue this conversation until we reach the clinic, and then I say goodbye and hand the phone back to my husband. A group of women walk past as I climb from the auto-rickshaw. They cackle with laughter. *A lucky girl managed to escape being his wife. If she did, I can too.* I smile at the retreating backs of the women.

* *

The doctor wants to know how long we have been married. She wants to know the date of my last period. Not regular, it is as moody as I am. She prescribes birth-control pills. My husband freaks out. 'We are trying to have a baby. We want a baby. Do you understand?'

The doctor remains calm. 'This is to regularize her periods. She cannot conceive unless her calendar is in place.'

He remains defiant and asks her to find a way where I don't have to take these tablets. 'Hormones never did anyone any good.' So, the doctor amicably opts out, and sings the virtues of multi-vitamins and folic acid. Having a baby is only a matter of discussion between the doctor and the husband. The woman does not ask me if I want a baby, if I am ready for a baby, if I am happy with my husband, if I have any problems that I might want to discuss. She asks him to take me to a medical centre for a scan so that she can decide the further course of treatment.

Violence is not something that advertises itself. It is not written on my face – he is too careful for that, of course, aiming his fists at my body. As long as a woman cannot speak, as long as those to whom she speaks do not listen, the violence is unending.

* *

My mother on the phone:
A child is not a bad idea. He will become more gentle when

197

he is a father. I'm a mother. Babies have that effect, they can tame brutes.

When you have a child, try to move back to Chennai. There will be an element of control. We can intervene. He cannot carry on in this fashion here. Right now he is on an ego-trip. He will eventually climb down. When he looks at the face of a child, he cannot beat the mother as he pleases. When the child grows up, it will tell him to get lost if he raises his hand against you. Anyway, if he's beating you, it only shows he has run out of arguments. Just be patient, dear. Buy yourself time, bring him here. Please do not lose hope. Do not act in haste. Take care.

* *

The man's fluids form the bones. The woman's fluids form the flesh. This is the belief of elders in my ancestral village. This is how they think life begins. I do not think they have got it wrong at all. They just do not know that when a child forms inside the womb of a sad, broken woman, its little heart will be made up of her tears.

* *

Mangalore's oppressive heat at noon. A heat that will not subside until the sky tears itself into a thousand pieces and begins to rain down.

I reach the medical centre. I have had the recommended

two glasses of water. When I meet my husband in the waiting room, he presents me with a tender coconut, full of milk. It is not a gift but a precaution. My name is called for the pelvic exam and the doctor positions me under the machine, but after several moments of button pushing and sighing, he sends me back saying the quantity of the water in me is still insufficient for the machine to light up my insides.

My husband is furious. He calls up my father and weeps to him. 'Your daughter has new-fangled ideas. She thinks she is Miss World. She wants to maintain her figure. She does not drink water. She does not want to have my children.'

He fetches a two-litre bottle of water from the reception and orders me to drink it. I put the neck to my lips and tip the bottle. 'Faster,' he orders, lifting the bottle to a sharper angle. '*Faster.*' Halfway through I wrench the bottle away, gasping for air. I tell him I cannot take it anymore, that I'm going to drown. He slaps me in front of everyone. The people in the waiting room either watch or avert their eyes. To them, this is just an overexcited man eager to be a father. They do not know what I live through. Or maybe they all know, and everyone takes it for granted. Or everyone believes, like I sometimes do, that the next day would be better.

I put the bottle to my mouth again and drink. Almost immediately, I feel nauseous and before long I'm vomiting water down my chest. He is disgusted. 'Imagine this is a literary festival. Imagine this nurse is Arundhati Roy. Imagine these people are some of your fucking writers. Will you throw up then? Hold it in. Behave yourself. You have no responsibility. You have no intention of being either a wife or a mother. Thousands of women have scans every day, but the only one making a scene is you. You want to keep your size zero frame. You are a zero yourself. You do not want my children. You will be out of business as a whore if you become a mother. Why do you torture me?'

* *

He is right. I do not want his baby. I cannot bring a baby into a world in which I have no love. I do not want to bring into the world a son who will watch his mother being beaten up, I do not want to bring into the world a daughter who will be beaten up.

When my scan is over, the doctor compliments me on having such a loving husband; on being married to such a devoted, doting man, the lecturer who takes a long lunch break so that he can be by the side of his wife when she is undergoing an ultrasound of her pelvis.

At no time does he give me an opportunity to talk to him. At no time does he ask me how I am. Even if he had, how could I open up to strangers who buy the fiction performed for their benefit?

We appear helpless in front of doctors and they heal us. They protect us. Perhaps there was a part of me that had

believed that doctors would protect me, would stop this en-
forced fertility treatment, would come to my rescue. It is only
now, finally, that I realize that if I want to be rescued, I'll have
to do it myself.

* *

My skills in the kitchen are summoned forth in my secret
plan of foiling Project Baby. The breakfast chutneys for the
dosa that I make no longer contain only groundnuts, green
chillies and onion, but I toss in a spoon of white sesame
seeds. I follow the whispers of teenaged years, when girls with
delayed periods, girls who had sex without condoms, girls
who were married early kept motherhood at bay with kitchen
ingredients. In my fish curry, the tang comes not from tomato
or tamarind – I introduce the pulp of raw, green mangoes
into the spicy gravy. My grandmother's recipe, I maintain
to my husband, rejoicing in the forbidden knowledge that
the heat-inducing mango will forestall the possibility of
conception. Every dish is destiny. Even fruits I choose for
a post-dinner snack are not innocent. I serve diced papayas
sprinkled with black salt and paprika, slices of pineapple with
brown sugar. These are the fruits that are kept out of reach of
pregnant women for fear of miscarriage. This is how I turn
my kitchen into a combat zone, making sure that my cooking
secures my and my womb's liberty.

* *

One night, having endured my husband's attentions in bed, I stumble to the bathroom to pee. No sooner have I sat on the toilet seat than he forces his way through the door and kicks me to the floor. He sees it as a systematic conspiracy to ensure that I never get pregnant, argues that I'm making every attempt to avoid having children, flushing out his seminal deposits as soon as he has fucked me. After that, every night of sex comes with an instruction to lie still on my back.

The one time I protest that I do actually need to go to the toilet is followed, the next evening, with the directive to go and get rid of all my fucking piss and all my fucking shit before we go to bed.

Protestations are seen as eternally damning proofs that I do not want to embrace motherhood. In his lexicon, not conceiving his child is one million times more outrageous than my previous avatar of being a petit-bourgeois poet-prostitute. My crime of being lackadaisical about giving birth to his heir is seen as a conspiracy to end his bloodline. In his mind, it equals a genocide.

* *

'I've killed three people. Three, not one or two. One of them wasn't even a soldier. Now I'm telling you so that you know me for real. So, yes, look into my eyes. Face me. Here, this knife. Do you feel it. Cold, yes. It will be warm in a second when I slash your throat. Sad, isn't it? The knife will not know you are a famous writer.'

* *

It is essential to act like a woman he can trust.

It is essential to give him the feeling of, if not quite being loved, at least respected. It is essential to throw him off the scent so that I can begin to plot my escape. It is essential to pretend that I'm eager for motherhood. Because I have left him countless times in my mind, I find it easy to essay this role, for I now know how a woman who is leaving will behave and so I know how to play the opposite.

* *

The coming of the New Year brings with it the opportunity to make easy promises. I swear to him that I will turn over a new leaf. I tell him: this is the brand new beginning. At first, it is a made-in-Mangalore, manufactured happiness that I wrap around the two of us. I give up all the constructs of being a writer, a woman who has a thought, a woman with a life outside Primrose Villa. The daily news is what he tells me. Communication is restricted to the calls that he allows me to answer, only in his presence. Emails are only those I hear about through him. I wash my hair with the dirt-green bar of bathing soap, respecting his oft-repeated story about the austerity of comrades. When I develop lice and dandruff, I pretend not to notice. Domesticity binds us together. In the creator's handbook, this is the mandatory calm that has to be orchestrated before an impending storm. In the more rustic world of my ancestors, this is the ceremonial bathing and garlanding of the sacrificial goat, a token display of affection before the axe falls.

Peacetime lets me take a step back, to become the writer again, to closely observe my protagonists in laboratory conditions, note the changes in their behaviour. Peacetime lulls him into a zone of comfort, makes it easier for me to catch him off-guard. Peacetime allows me to plot. I collect together every scrap of information that I know about him. I fill in the blanks of his story. In my spare time, I read up on narratives of Naxalites, to build a profile of those who leave the organization: state agents, deserters, informers, cowards – I place my husband in two of these boxes. I try to decipher a pattern to our previous fights. I want to test my hunch about the duration of calm and the inversely proportional extent of explosiveness in the inevitable clash. I make mental lists of his possible triggers of violence. I also make lists of his favourite topics of conversation.

* *

My husband rejoices in the change in me. He sees it as validation of all his criticisms and corrections. Jubilation quickly gives way to tenderness, a sharing of his stories, a retreat that allows me access to his vulnerability.

Stories about a disciplinarian father in the Army who came home only on holidays. About a summer of jaundice, and how his mother nursed him back to health. Bitter anecdotes of the rabble-rousing he had done in his workplaces. A shape-shifting story of how often he jumped across party lines – Marxist to Marxist-Leninist to People's War to Maoist. Growing from leftist to radical to underground guerrilla, getting more extremist every step of the way. In the middle of all the adventurism, the dreams of the children he wants to have, the names he wants to give them, the places he wants to take them on holiday.

Pity seems possible; I have a compulsive need to dole it out like small change, but the writer in me is stronger than the woman in me. One evening, when I'm setting up the rainy day snack of masala tea and freshly made onion *pakoras*, he comes up to the kitchen holding a pair of trousers that have long been left untouched and undisturbed in the wardrobe; he tells me that they belonged to a friend, a comrade, who was shot dead when their Western Ghats squad came under fire. He brings the dead man's trousers reverentially to his eyes, and then he clutches them against his chest. I'm making mental notes, sketching out the narrative as he speaks. I ask him if he saw his friend die, if anyone else was there, if they tried to save him. It hurts him to talk about it, but I also feel that he is desperate to share the details with someone. I only have to allow the story to unspool. *Did you manage to retrieve his body? Oh no, did you leave your dying friend there because you wanted to save your own lives? That must have been horrible. I know it is not your fault. No, it is not your mistake, my dear. I know why you blame yourself for it. Were you sure he was at least dead? What if the police tortured him later on? Did they at least give back the body?* He is crying, gasping for breath, in his effort to fill me in with the details. His voice breaks but my resolve to drive him into despair has not been broken yet. I have gently talked him into a ball on the floor, weeping and hitting his head, hugging the trousers to his chest.

I am amazed how indifferent I can be. As he falls apart at my feet, I simply watch, still taking notes, making numbered observations. 1) It is possible to play with him emotionally, to push him into distress, into anger, into anywhere I want him to go. 2) A pair of trousers makes a great prop.

This is how the writer in me takes charge. What if someone were to choose to make a film about a courageous young fighter suffering the legacy of PTSD? What could they place in his hands? What is one of the few things that will not take away his masculinity and at the same time showcase his vulnerability? *Trousers.*

This is my line of thought. I am already transferring what I see and experience in the privacy of our home into art. I have put myself in a dangerous situation with this marriage, but even in this complicated position, I'm finding plot points.

This is the occupational hazard of being a writer-wife.

* *

The suspicious, violent husband is a character, but already, just by being who he is, he is becoming the first semblance of a plot. It's a plot that goes nowhere except in dizzying circles, and it's a plot that remains tightly under his control. But, recently, I have begun to learn how to wrest it back – first, in my experiment with silence that ended in the surprising plot twist of corrective, disciplinary rape; the last time, in the episode of the trousers.

I remind myself of the fundamental notion of what it means to be a writer. A writer is the one who controls the narrative.

* *

In the Marxist jargon that I have studiously picked up from my husband, I can proudly declare: there are tactics, and then, there is strategy.

I have become a strategist.

I indulge in picking over the delicious detail of the episode with the trousers. I remember that my defiance over the trip to the gynaecologist was enough to make him inflict burns on his own body with a glowing ladle. I begin to realize, for the first time, that his violence, which is forever directed against me, can sometimes be twisted to turn upon himself.

It gives me hope. I know that his anger is a device that I can detonate at will. When the right time comes, I can push the red button, I can conclude this classic, kitchen-sink drama on my own terms.

* *

I decide that I will not allow myself to be portrayed as the hot-blooded woman who ran away from one man into the wide open arms of another. I will not allow myself to become the good wife, the good mother, the good-for-nothing woman that marriage aims to reduce me to. I will not allow my story to become a morality tale – about loose women, about lonely writers, about melancholic poets, about creative, unstable artists, not even about a war against head lice. I will give all of you an ending to this story to which you cannot object. I will hold out until I hand-deliver the finishing thread that will earn your teary-eyed, hard-won approval – a return to my parental home, to that state of innocence, to a system of returning.

To my parents, caught in the self-fulfilling prophecy of exemplary citizenship, I will bequeath to them the wounded pride they seek. When I come home battered, running to save my life, they can remind the neighbours just how hard we all tried to save my marriage, but just the fact that they are having me back is proof positive that I have done something right, or, my husband has done something unspeakably wrong.

I phone them to prepare the way. I get the courage to share the shame of how I have been treated, what it means to live in the fear of being killed. I repeat my husband's threat to scalp me word for word. I talk of my death. I cradle the menacing words like a militant's hand grenade and pull the pin. 'Next time he talks of murder, come home,' my mother implores. 'If he does it again, run for your life without even turning to look back,' my father orders. 'We are here,' they say, finally, far too late, but in unison.

* *

Until then, I stay. I stay because I have no other choice until I am within touching distance of a permitted resolution. In the eyes of the world, a woman who runs away from death is more dignified than a woman who runs away from her man. She does not face society's stone-throwing when she comes away free. In the quest to control the narrative, I still have to endanger my own life.

* *

'Whoever said you will walk out of this marriage?'

It's raining outside. The sky is dull, the falling light of an early January evening. I've no energy to answer. I bury my head on his chest. I hate him, but, so close to the end, I feel a writer's sense of sadness at ending a character. He puts his hands around my shoulders, kisses me on the forehead.

'We've proved them all wrong, no? We're inseparable. No force can come between us. Those who said that you're not marriage-material and only fit for one-night stands will have to eat their own words. You are my lovely wife. My perfect wife. I didn't believe we'd end this way. Just look at us now. We're perfect.'

* *

In the kitchen, I am shelling green peas and chopping up mushrooms and capsicum. I make a curry with aubergines and green chillies. The rice dances in the boiling water. I drain the rice, and set it aside. When I check, every grain is standing up as if in prayer. I call my husband to eat. He is busy marking answer sheets. Just then, a phone call shows up on my phone. It is a missed call. Then another. Then another. It is almost as if someone is playing a joke. He demands that I tell him who this secret caller is. It is a number I do not know, I do not recognize. When we call back, the person on the other end answers the phone, remains silent, ends the call. My husband rings that number again and again, and shouts into the plastic handset. Soon, the mystery phone is switched off, sending him through to an automated answerphone every time he dials. It upsets him. He turns towards me and demands to know who it is. He begins enumerating my past lovers, demanding to know if I have gone back to fucking the politician, questioning if I'm once more involved with an old university boyfriend. He tells me I disgust him; that I pollute him with my history; that I am not good enough for him; that I am once again ruining our marriage.

I see my chance and sharpen the blade.

'But darling,' I say quietly, 'why all this hypocrisy? It is you who already has one failed marriage behind him.'

I slip the words between his ribs like a stiletto knife. He actually gasps. His eyes widen. For the first time since I met him, he has no response. And as I watch him, trying to give shape to his confusion, I know I have won. His open hand slams into my throat and tightens. He hoists me up against the wall, holding me by my neck alone. My legs dangle. I cannot breathe. My mind is on an endless chant: *This will end this will end this will end this will end.*

'Death scares you. That is the difference between me and you. I'm not afraid of death. I can kill, but in the same breath, I can die. Both are the same to me. Not to you. You are hungry, greedy, begging for life. Look at you now. Scared. I can only laugh at you. Look at you. You will never, ever be a revolutionary.'

He takes his hand away and I collapse. My lungs heave and struggle for air, but when I catch my breath I look up at him and defiantly smile. My voice finds it difficult to escape my crushed throat, but the words I need begin composing

211

themselves into perfect sentences; they find their way, painfully, like the angry cry of an animal that watches another being slaughtered; forcefully, like rain-bearing wind searing itself through palm fronds. My heart beats in my throat to the rhythm of imagined machine gun fire.

'Revolutionary? They shot your friend dead, and you abandoned his body to the enemy. Don't pretend you are a revolutionary. Don't tell me how brave you are. A brave man doesn't run. A brave man doesn't rape and hit his wife. You, my husband, are not a brave man.'

I exceed my written brief. He shouts and screams at me as he pins me to the floor of the living room, but I no longer hear him. He is holding my face down with his foot, his toes digging into my cheeks, stamping on my ears. This is how he demands my silence. I see his lips form words – whore, bitch, cunt, pros-ti-tute – but his voice no longer reaches me. On the floor, my hands clenching his ankles, I look like a woman offering prayers, like someone pleading for her life. The blows rain down on me and then, finally, the ringing in my ears is broken by the phrase I have been waiting for: 'I am going to bring this to an end. Now. You are going to die. I should have done this long ago.'

For the first time in my marriage, I'm not afraid. I know that my words have stripped away his manhood, they have shamed him into impotence. I know that my words have rendered him incapable of acting on his threat, and that now, in the space between us, there is his invisible cowardice that has been called out by name. But his verbal threat to kill is enough. It's what I came for. He is scripting the ending that I wanted for us. I generously allow him this authorship. He is dishing out the black and white version demanded by this world. I close my eyes and I wait for him to finish.

* *

All that I need, I carry with me in a shoulder bag. Passport. ATM card. Laptop. My phone that he never let me use. All of this is mine. This is all I could think of taking. This is all I had the time to take. This is all that I wanted to take.

I call home. I tell my mother I'm coming to her. Bruised but alive. The moon is on my back. The auto-rickshaw races into the night. I shed this miserable city like a second skin.

XIII

one thing I dont need
is any more apologies
i got sorry greetin me at my front door
you can keep yrs
i dont know what to do wit em
they dont open doors
or bring the sun back
they dont make me happy
or get a mornin paper

NTOZAKE SHANGE,
FOR COLORED GIRLS WHO HAVE CONSIDERED
SUICIDE/WHEN THE RAINBOW IS ENUF

For four months and eight days I had been off every radar. No phone, no email, not even the curated happiness of Facebook.

No news is bad news, but most people do not know it yet.

Did anyone ask for me?

A friend says he assumed my silence was a need for privacy. That things were going well and that I had dug myself deep into the land with my new husband, and to call me or to track me down would disturb me and that I would climb out of my little warren when I felt the need to feel the sun on my face.

We thought that no news is good news.

We thought that you wanted the space.

We thought you would call us when you were ready.

We emailed you, your husband replied saying you'll write to us soon.

We thought you were out of Facebook as you were busy with that project, no?

And everywhere, people only encountered normal-ness, an ordinary state of being, the absence of any trouble, because that's what they had set out to find.

* *

I am considered lucky to have walked out of a bad marriage in four months. I am considered too unlucky to be invited to friends' weddings, as if my embittered and embattled aura will pull apart the four-poster bridal beds.

You cannot always have it all, baby.

* *

Even after hearing my story, women hide their husbands from me.

You'd think it would upset me, make me ponder on female rivalry and insecurity. No. I'm thankful for small mercies. I once had a husband I wanted to hide from the world, too.

* *

In place of a firing squad, I stare down the barrels of endless interrogation.

Why did she not run away?

Why did she not use the opportunities that she had for escape?

Why did she stay if, indeed, the conditions were as bad as she claims?

How much of this wasn't really consensual?

Let me tell you a story. Not mine, this time around.

It is the story of a girl we call after the place of her birth, lacking the integrity to even utter her name. The Suryanelli Girl.

Forty-two men rape this girl, over a period of forty days.

She is sixteen years old.

The police do not investigate her case. The high court questions her character. The highest court in the land asks the inevitable. Why did she not run away? Why did she not use the opportunities that she had for escape? Why did she stay if, indeed, the conditions were as bad as she claims? How much of this wasn't *really* consensual?

Sometimes the shame is not the beatings, not the rape.

The shaming is in being asked to stand to judgment.

* *

I am not the damsel-in-distress. I am not the picture of virginal innocence, someone whose parents hitched her to a man in an arranged marriage. This is the kind of thing that can happen to a helpless woman like that.

But I am not that. I am rough, gruff, tough. The one who has written these mad and angry and outrageous poems about life and love and sex.

I am not afraid of men; I have fashioned myself in the defiant image of its exact, uncompromising opposite – the woman men are afraid of. I am anti-fragile. I've been made not to break. That is one of the reasons why it becomes harder to talk about the violence. Who I am proves to be my own undoing.

Is this happening to you? The disbelief.

Did you let this happen to you? The shock.

Why did you put up with all of this? The shame.
You knew better, didn't you? The shame, again.
Why did you not reach out to one of us? The lack of trust.
If only we had known…

It does not cross their mind that a woman who is being beaten is intimidated into feeling, believing, knowing that to ask for help from others will only put her at greater risk. In their questions and their responses I come to know that even those of them who have mastered the theory have not lived through the experience: they lack the insight that a woman being abused can mostly trust only one person for help. Herself.

* *

Not having a man in my life now becomes a series of little activities and rituals. I replace men with an array of placeholders.

A blank page. Poetry, in translation, rife with awkward, charming metaphors. Reading the funny below-the-line comments that follow a sober article. Girl crushes. The supreme sense of accomplishment derived from preparing a meal just for myself. The mushrooms browning in butter, and for a little time, a sharp smell that reminds me of sex.

A cat, any cat, because at the moment I lack self-confidence and I am badly in need of some basic lessons in independence and attitude. Raiding the clothes cupboards of my friends. Long skirts. Bead necklaces. Mismatched, dangling earrings and the courage to wear them in public. Compliments from strangers on the road.

Watching peacock feathers grow a little between the pages of my diary, choreographing the waltz of iron filings with a magnet held beneath the paper, pressing flowers into heavy books, trying to tie-dye a *dupatta*.

Elfriede Jelinek and Clarice Lispector. Women writing women in the way in which I might someday write myself.

Long volatile emails with numbered lists and half-formed poems. Colourful curses, damning every man to hell and halfway back. The perverse pleasure of rejecting all advances, even from the men I am attracted to because I am in no mood to create that kind of space at this point in my life. Wearing the same rust-red tunic for three days to hold all my energy from leaving me. Two-hour-long showers and soap bubbles.

Sleep.

Reading Calvin and Hobbes endlessly. Wishing I had a little son exactly like Calvin. The undeniable urge to adopt all of the beautiful children I see. Loving my mother, in spite of everything, because she managed to keep me whole. Loving my father, in spite of everything, because he cared for me when I came home broken.

Compulsive anorexia, or the desire to achieve the waist-lines of chola bronzes.

Imagining myself as the widow of each of the men I've dated (and especially the one I married), and grieving in accordance with how much I loved them while it lasted. Falling to my knees to weep for their deaths. Beating my breast. Wearing black. Wearing white. Wearing nothing but wine-red lipstick, because some men need to be remembered that way.

Mirrors. Scream-crying, shy-smiling in their presence. The monologues, the dialogues, the disorienting impermanence of playing out life for the benefit of a one-woman audience. The soul-talk where I congratulate myself on every moment that I do not have to bother about the incorrigible nature of love, its heavy baggage and bitter arguments, the needless questions of men, the worthless jealousy of other women.

The conversation that I never have, but always rehearse within my head: I am a tough bitch, I can take it, I am happy you asked me if you could help. I did not deserve this sadness. I do not know if I deserve all this love, either.

The resignation of my mind's million anxieties when I begin to run. The defiant straightness of my shoulders that catches me by surprise. My wild hair, with a life of its own, where my lovers have buried their kisses and their prayers.

Last of all, the world of the books I enter, the world that I create in writing, the word-tunnels that I burrow, where I bury myself.

* *

I write a first-person account of the marriage for a magazine. Hundreds of women write in to say that in the thousand and odd words of my piece, they feel their stories, their voices, their tears. A woman from Australia recounts how her friend, a victim of domestic violence, was killed on 10 January 2012. It was the same day that my husband pinned me to the wall and threatened to kill me. The day I left. The coincidence is eerie.

In the days that follow, I wake up to social media unpicking every single thread of my life. The post-mortem analysis of my marriage reveals more about people and their prejudices than anything about me or my husband. Quick to condemn, they say my abuser is Sri Lankan Tamil, a Dalit, a Christian. He is none of the above. It is a short-cut to absolve larger society of blame and to make those that are marginalized into the mischief-makers.

The worst attacks blame me. What kind of feminist was she? Why did she endure it for four months? Is this a publicity stunt? And then the poser: if she was indeed abused why does she weep to the national media, why does she not go to the police? If she was indeed abused, why doesn't she report the abuser? Trial by media is no trial, her husband must be proved guilty in a court of law. If she is a feminist, why does she let her rapist and abuser walk away scot-free?

I might have moved from Mangalore, from the marriage, but I realize that I cannot get away from abuse. To save face, and in the hope of justice, I turn over the corpse of my marriage to the police. I meet lawyers, I pay consultation fees with a writer's unsteady, meagre income.

* *

I realize that penance does not finish with the act of nailing myself to a cross. To suffer for the sins of this world, there is much more to be endured. To those who know only the public persona, I will not be vindicated until I have knocked on every door of justice, until I have sent the culprit to prison, until I have endlessly relived my tragedy through the filing of petitions and complaints and depositions and a sensational series of cases that begin to proliferate around me, stretching from one city to the next. To those who know me personally, it becomes my responsibility to wipe their tears, to ameliorate their sorrows surrounding the unfortunate events of my marriage, to make them feel that somehow it was all better than how it has been portrayed.

Almost a year after I walked away from the marriage, I visit a Tamil friend's house. I'm playing with my friend's son, his wife's tidying up around us, he's getting ready to go to work. This is the third and last day of my visit.

'I read what you've written about your marriage.'

He's referring to the article I wrote for the magazine.

'Okay.'

'It's sad.'

'Sure.'

'What you went through is horrible. I'm not disputing it.'

'Okay. So?'

'Just that this man whom you depicted – it was like he was a monster. The sum total of all the evil things in the world.'

'No, I never said that.'

'But that's how it came across.'

'That's not what I intended. It was his violence. That's all.'

Here's a friend asking me if there was nothing redeemable about my ex-husband. I do not know how to justify myself. What do I tell people like him, who want a balanced picture, who want to know that this was a real person with a rainbow side, just so that they are reminded of their own humanity?

I realize that this is the curse of victimhood, to feel compelled to lend an appropriate colour of goodness to their abuser. *Forgive them, Father, for they know not what they do.* The landlord's benevolence, the overseer's kindness, the criminal's humour, the wife-beater's punctuality.

He made the best *rasam* I've ever tasted. He sang out of tune always, but with no hint of shyness. That sometimes, when he was not angry, or proud, I saw him with a lost look in his eyes. He dimpled when he smiled. He yearned for his mother's approval – but for some reason he never got it. His father, a major in the Indian Army, had beaten him often as a child. He had made a note of it every time it happened in a small pocketbook. It was easy to believe that a little love would make him whole again. I had convinced myself to believe that when everything told me I was wrong.

He was given to white lies. But I knew he loved me. That was not one of his lies. He could walk for hours on end with no sign of tiredness. He did not know what to do when we went to Ullal beach – the two of us, alone in the open, under an unforgiving afternoon sun, he looked hopeless, almost out of place. There was nothing romantic about him, and that was endearing.

When we were in the presence of people he did not know, people who did not matter to his career or his politics – and this included my parents – he spoke without a pause to me, as if from a fear that if he stopped to breathe, I would use that pause in his throat to wander away, as if his speech was a snare, as if it was all he had to stop me from leaving him behind.

* *

My husband was the only man I left. Before I was married, it was the men who left me. Afterward, in my life as a divorcee, they started leaving me again.

I know now how to read its onset. Overnight, their eyes go into exile. When they wake up, their eyes wear the open disinterest of strangers. Yet the men remain a while longer, until they cannot bear the familiar itch of their feet and then they are gone.

* *

Some men leave me with memories, a secret language, unfinished poems, frayed old T-shirts, half-told anecdotes of their childhood, newspaper clippings in a script I cannot read, books defaced with dog-ears and underlinings, swearwords, a taste for grunge singers, abandoned promises of holiday plans.

Some men keep it minimal: jangling regrets in their pockets with their car keys, hurrying to the door and leaving me with a final, clumsy love bite. I wear it on my skin for a week at the most, until it fades away along with the dreams we shared.

Some men leave me with a thousand kisses, but these kisses are contagious, and once I have caught them, it is a curse – they keep me awake, feverish, I cannot sleep night after night after night.

Some men leave me with unresolved fights and I ache in anger, never being able to apologize, or feel vindicated, and I have to live the rest of my life like a student with a failed grade, with a bulleted list of points that I cannot make, or concede.

Some men leave me because it is a matter of routine for them – refusing to give or take blame, just putting the sad turn of events down to time, or place, or luck, or stress, or stars, or jobs, or their respective, respectable families.

Some men leave me even as they are with me, knowing

227

that I will never be able to love them the way their mothers loved them, and that they will never be able to love me the way they love themselves. Some men leave me because of this absence of deference, and because they are not used to living in a space that is not a dedicated shrine, where they are not considered divine.

Some men leave me because I am unpredictable – sunshine one moment and storm clouds the next; the scent of summer rain with the sleep-depriving aftershock of thunder. They cannot keep pace with the fighting that follows the kissing that follows the argument that follows the laughing in unending circles.

Some men leave me because they have the misplaced confidence that they can always pick me up later in life, pluck me from wherever I have put down roots and replant me in the shade of what they have to offer.

Some men leave me in the middle of a long kiss, tongue and lips working mechanically, while their minds race with business goals, PowerPoint presentations, office politics, political office, the crisis of capitalism, the sister's marriage, the repayments on the car loan, terrorism, the bills to pay, the new waitress who has smiled often enough to be taken seriously, the last ex-girlfriend who has started sending ambiguous signals over the past week, the next day's plans, misplaced objects and the fervent anticipation of a beep-beep on their phone.

Some men leave me just as soon as they have come. Others, only after we have experimented our way together through the *Kamasutra*, and my body has contorted itself into every shape that their porn-directed desire demands, and now sex with me holds no novelty, so they move on, to women who are more portable, more flexible, more young, and crucially, more naive.

Some men leave me before anything even begins between us, because they are terrified that I use small words like *cage* and *consent* in an exaggerated political fashion, and being a writer I spell trouble, and if they had half a chance they would magic me into stone or turn me into a pillar of salt, but being kind and gentle, they remove themselves from my presence.

Some men leave me silently because I make the mistake of telling them that other men have been kinder, but in their minds, this is already rejection-through-comparison because they assume that kinder translates to better, and better translates to (what else?) better-in-bed, and better-in-bed translates into the larger size of other men's penises, and that competition actually translates into a belittling, almost a castration, and no man wants to enter that no-man's land.

Some men leave me because they have just met another woman who does not wield her words like Molotovs, who creates better monochrome memories, who holds permissible quantities of bitterness, who knows her place and who sings their praise.

Some men leave me because they have no other options left, they leave me because my eyes no longer light up with love and it breaks them to see that they have broken me.

* *

In the meantime, the quest for justice does not lead anywhere.

Picture the red-brick ramshackle inside of an Indian police station. Petty criminals sitting along the floors of corridors with their hands folded over their knees. Wooden benches reserved for the more respectable visitors. Bleached ceiling fans with years of gathered cobwebs, making a grudging noise every turn they make. An old constable stretching like a cat in the sun before his afternoon nap, a fixture as old as the rest of the furniture. Telephones and wireless sets and heaps of paperwork on every table. A computer in the corner, reserved for use by the youngest and only tech-savvy officer. Within this scene of everyday chaos, a partitioned area for women. An obese female police inspector looks through pictures of my marriage and asks me what is my husband's height (six feet and two inches) and mine (five feet and an inch). She suggests there is little compatibility. 'Why did you marry him?' she asks with a smirk. 'Did you expect a big cock?' She looks at me with a level, mocking gaze. I don't respond. Shame comes in many flavours. This one is meant to be swallowed silently.

She berates my mother for not giving a dowry to my

husband. Men who marry a girl for a dowry treat her nicely. Men who marry her for other reasons, well, *this* is how it ends.

Then the inevitable question: love or arranged marriage? I don't know quite how to answer. Love and arranged marriage, I suppose. I repeat the summary of my story. We met on Facebook. I was part of a campaign against the death penalty. We had mutual friends. We consulted each other to draft statements. It turned into friendship. I opened up to him. He appeared principled, sincere and enormously respectful. The arguments always polite, political. I saw no intention to flirt, to breach the boundaries of our comradeship. It was a space in which I felt safe. I trusted him enough to tell him what I thought. We made plans for the future. I was single, heartbroken. I did not want any fooling around. He offered to marry me. At that time, it was all I wanted to hear from a man. Not really love. Not really arranged. Where do we cast the in-betweens?

She married in haste. She unmarried in haste. She rushed into it, she rushed out of it. I understand those who judge.

* *

I write letters to St Alfonso College in Mangalore. There's an internal review and a quick, short response. 'We will ask him to resign.'

Demanding a man's resignation, instead of terminating his services, is the short-cut academic institutions like to take. Sacking an abusive faculty member involves process, procedure, a committee, its findings, the decision, his appeal. A resignation is easier from the institution's point of view – the problem sorts itself out. The problem merely packs its bags and goes to another town and sets up shop. A different university, a different city, a different set of references. As long as this man is not their headache, everyone at the old place is unconcerned about this new arrangement. This is how he shape-shifts and moves around. College to college, city to city, country to country.

He moves to Chennai, becomes an English lecturer at the Tambaram Christian College. I ask the college board why they shelter him. Well, what happened with you is personal, they say. *Personal.*

Then, he moves to South Africa. He champions a wide range of causes. A paper on the importance of mother-tongue education for the Zulu and Indian people. The necessity for safe, violence-free homes in Durban and community support for affected women. The recording of oral histories of indentured labourers in order to put together a narrative of their bondage and suffering. The popular Palestinian cause. Riding on the wave of anti-imperialist sentiment, he even endorses ISIS as a counter to American war-mongering. Activism becomes the mask behind which he hides. He plays the race card when this or that supervisor complains about whichever stance he might be taking. There is no end to his chameleonism. His fields of expertise are inclusive sexuality and masculinity. This is not hypocrisy, this is sophisticated multidisciplinary mutation. The messianic status conferred on him for picking up the causes of the dispossessed allows him to entrench himself into communities. At this stage, talking about his misogyny, his violence, becomes an act of blasphemy against a crusader.

For two and a half years, my case at the Metropolitan Magistrate Court fails to be called. I run from pillar to post. I want him to come to India and face charges – if he takes citizenship elsewhere, then I can hardly run to Interpol.

Important Communist writers act as intermediaries and say that I must remain silent about him. A journalist comes to my home asking me to accept financial compensation. The Additional Public Prosecutor, who is tasked with defending me, asks me if I'm jealous of his new girlfriend. That's the man who is going to argue my case on behalf of the state.

Then there is the divorce petition, sent by his lawyers, which talks about my ultra-feminism, which blames my parents for my modern upbringing. Forgetting everything seems a forlorn, unattainable dream. Years after you walk out, you will still be caught in the web of a bad marriage.

* *

Those closest to me bear the brunt. My mother copes by flamboyantly chronicling my medical ailments for her friends. Sadly, my father cannot match her imaginative or narrative powers.

He matches her in nearly everything else – educational qualifications, being a government servant, his take-home salary, voting DMK, being an early morning person, haggling over the price of vegetables, a preference for cardamom in tea, face-reading, the ability to come up with soulful renderings of *Bharathiyar* and word-for-word quotations from Shakespeare and absolutely original Tamil swearwords, and a marked tendency to observe superstitions and self-medicate.

Unlike my mother's tendency to resort to graphic descriptions of her own battle to bring me back into human society, my father handles the problem of my hasty marriage and hastier unmarriage in an extremely methodical manner.

When people ask him what his daughter is doing, he makes an instant estimate of how close the interrogator is to the family. Auto-rickshaw drivers, distant neighbours, distant relatives get a sanitized version of my being happily married and living in America or Singapore or London or whatever city is in vogue that month. In my father's story tailored to Tier One (Strangers), I live the life of expat contentment, my husband teaches at a prestigious university, and our couple is a happy Double-Income-No-Kids unit, in a home full of gadgets to do our every bidding, and the only reason the son-in-law is not seen in Chennai is because of green-card obligations or he is working on a book and does not find the time to travel.

In the story spun for those in Tier Two (Influential Strangers) – which encompasses work colleagues, neighbours, police officers, college principals, and people to whom he is prone to run for help in the case of misfortune – his daughter is back home 'at the moment' because there was 'a little misunderstanding' and 'time heals' and 'absence makes the heart grow fonder' and 'you know how it is with young people these days'.

Then there is the non-story customized for the Tier Three (Annoying Acquaintances) audience, a category that comprises shared friends of both father and daughter, usually arranged as tiles on a Facebook wall. This is the category of people that knows more about my taste in coffee and clothes than he does, that knows that I was last logged on from [insert name of café/pub], this is the category that secretly wonders whether the glass I'm holding in Profile Photo dated dd/mm/yyyy contains Coca-Cola, or is liberally mixed with JD, and this is the category that knows the names of the men who generously like all my posts. This is also the category that is the most heterogeneous, a group as assorted as the one you might encounter at the Koyambedu bus-stand, including my father's once-upon-a-time Mathematics tutor, a respectable seventy-five-year-old man who one day angrily called up my father to complain that I had uploaded a picture in which my bra strap was visible on my shoulder. When my mother was consulted, she nonchalantly remarked that of course a girl's bra strap was meant to be on her shoulder, where else would it be?, and more importantly why was an old man spending his time on Facebook looking at the bra strap of a girl he had last met in the flesh when she was barely two years old?

Whenever my father assumes that the person across from him belongs to Tier Three, he ensures that the word daughter or children or offspring (or any of its synonyms) does not enter the conversation, and in the event that it does, and the inevitable questions follow, he has a stock answer: 'You tell me. You tell me what she is up to. She has grown up and got wings. There is only so much a father can be involved in his child's life.'

Tier Four (Friends, Family and Well-Wishers), as a category, are people who know much more about the story of my unfortunate marriage than necessary, and these are the ones who fault him for bringing up a headstrong daughter, for educating her too much, for bringing her up like a son, for not disciplining her enough, for sending her to study away from home without any supervision, for allowing this whirlwind marriage to take place, for not consulting them when the whirlwind marriage started to blow itself out, and for being a hen-pecked husband who listens too much to his wife and daughter. Tier Four are Emasculators Ltd. They are the ones my father is most afraid to face, and in response to all their reproofs, he merely nods his head and sighs: 'That girl N-E-V-E-R listened to me.'

* *

Long before I watched *Cinema Paradiso*, before I knew that Alfredo would angrily order Salvatore to leave the small town they call home, I had a similar directive from my father. *Go away. Don't come back.*

For many years, I couldn't understand why he would say such a thing to his own daughter, but then one evening, while sitting in my parents' living room, half watching the television and half rereading for the hundredth time the divorce petition, *Cinema Paradiso* provided the answer. *Go away. Don't come back.* It was an act of love. And so I finally followed his injunction. I moved as far away as my talent could take me.

Here, the sound of my hard heels on secluded cobblestone streets tells me that I have come far away, that I no longer need to run. The bare brown of trees stripped naked by winter. A cold that forces me to cover every inch of my skin. A stone-grey and moss-green local cemetery where I return myself to poetry. The dull sun in a cloudy sky, to be folded up and put away at the end of each day, to allow for faceless encounters in the night.

The first few weeks in a landscape completely altered from the familiar, I do nothing but soak up its… niceness.

237

I grow to like this new life, at once bereft of rage and intimacy. Here, I do not have a lover with whom I speak of a future. Here, I do not have a lover with whom I can share the lost words of my language. Here, I do not have a lover to whom I can write poems about the rain. Here, the rain itself is a nice stranger I do not want to know, not the intimate monsoon showers of home, with rolling thunders that crash-land at my window.

Here, the man across the room, the man I take to bed every night, the man I think I love can never unlock me, never access my mind, never splice my language open for me, never get down to the skin. I want him to remain a stranger. From experience, I know that it is easier to love strangers. I am willing to give this man my all, and, in the same instant, stay far away, out of reach. I want love, but I want it at an arm's distance, from where it cannot reach to hurt me.

This arrangement has its drawbacks. I do not tell him that I intend to stay. He does not ask me to leave. For the moment, we are wrapped up in niceness. A niceness that loves me.

A niceness that goes beyond him. This niceness where nobody asks me if I am married. This niceness without the dread of domestic violence. This niceness without the chokehold of marriage. This niceness where having three planets in my seventh house does not matter at all. This niceness, far away from home, a niceness that allows me to begin the process of forgetting and healing.

There is a poster of Marx above my lover's bed: *To be radical is to grasp things by the root*. I know that, in my case, to be radical means having to cut myself off at the root.

* *

A world made up in the dimension of my language is beautiful, but it also hides pain. This actual body of mine, I am ashamed and embarrassed and secretive about. My scars are my secrets. My straight shoulders sometimes slump; I wish my breasts would disappear. My hair falls out in handfuls, a shame like no other for a woman, one that can barely be admitted to even the closest of friends. Every hairstyle is a style to hide. My back hurts from sitting for long hours. I am a howling, screaming mess on the days of my period. My knees wear the rough defiance of a thousand kneel-down punishments at school. My cracked heels map the idea of a woman who does not have time for herself. I shave my legs depending on whether I am going to be with a lover that week, and only if that meeting holds the possibility of intimacy. The real body is militating against me, hurtling towards disease and age. I wear the battle wounds of heartbreak in my eyes. Whereas, the written body is completely under control. In the word-made-body, I am invincible. My breasts have the confidence of beauty queens. Men do not leave marks. Neither men as lovers, nor men as strangers.

My written body opens up only to the extent I decide to

demarcate. It does not require the permission of my parents, it does not require the approval of society. My words might reveal a generous cleavage, a breaking waist, but they do not let anyone put their hands on me. Wrapping my body into words, I proof it against the prying eye, against inspection. I have sheathed it against the hands of others. My woman's body, when it is written down, is rape resistant.

* *

Here, my flesh. Here, the haphazard lines of green running around my wrists. Here, my blood. Here, my jet black hair.

Wait. Here, my all-important cunt.

All muscle, all memory.

The only body I feel empowered to share is the body I fashion out of my own words. My skin acquires the right shade not in mirrors but when I write it down. Then, it is not fair or dark, it is not rough or glowing, it is not a skin that gets judged and condemned. It is skin on a woman like the bark on a tree. Brown, clearer under water, softer in the monsoon, brighter in sunshine, flaming in twilight.

My fingers, when captured in words, are poetry and song, music and dance, they trace little butterflies in the air. Behind words I hide the rough fingers of the girl who washes her clothes by hand every week; this is how I lead you away from the hands of an agitated, clumsy woman who spills sugar as she makes tea and spills the tea as she pours it out and breaks the cup when she attempts to clean up this mess. Words allow me escape. Words give birth to another woman.

* *

The trouble is, whenever I sit down to write about my marriage, his outbursts play in a loop. I've tailored playlists to help drown out his voice, but the music is already getting in the way of the writing – my fingers keep typing, but my ears focus on the lyrics. His reproaches superimpose themselves like a rap over the songs. M.I.A. meets Tom Waits meets moron ex-husband. *Hussel Hussel Hussel Grind Grind Grind A Whore Has Only One Thing On Her Mind.*

* *

I decide to leave his words in this book, where they belong.

Everything is writing material for you, isn't it? This marriage, this love, this dream I'm trying to build for the both of us.

Tomorrow, you'll be making a book out of it. There will be interviews and readings. You'll travel, pose for photographs, jumping across cities, jet-setting around the country, going to bed with any man you fancy that night. The writer. The free woman.

The trouble is that you do not want a decent chance at life. You're only after a story, and you make my life a living hell.

These words are the equivalent of an epitaph.

Underneath, a part of me lies buried.

XIV

I am the woman of myth and bullshit.
(True. I authored some of it.)

SANDRA CISNEROS, 'LOOSE WOMAN'

I am the woman sitting down to write her story. I am the woman preparing to arrest your attention. I am the woman being propped up for the world's inspection.

Here is my instruction manual:

Poke me in the eye. Pinch me in the waist. Note my height. Ask me to open my mouth wide. Shine a torch inside. Ask me to open my legs wide. Ask me to relax and breathe deeply. Shine a torch inside. Examine me: with your gloved fingers, with your speculum. Make notes. Laugh about me at lunch. See if you know somebody who knows somebody who knows somebody like me. They all do; all the time anyway. Come back because you have no other means of knowing me.

I am the woman who is a young writer with her pockets full of heavy stones, the one who has amassed sleeping tablets, the one with chiffon saris that will someday snap her neck. I am the glittering woman of puke and cowardice.

I am the woman who was a battered wife. I am the same wife who ran away.

I am the woman whose parentage is not probed. I am the

woman who does not provide evidence of lineage, the one who does not have to sketch my family tree with its mangled roots, with its share of concubines and kept women, with its incorrigible branches of bastardized children.

I am the woman who will not be silenced by the code of *sub judice* that forbids talk because judgment is pending. I am the woman accused of ultra-feminism in the divorce petition, the one who will not be shamed by the questions at the cross-examination. I am the one who does not sit around in family courts getting pulled up for the transgression of crossing her legs and not wearing her *thaali*.

I am the woman caught in the hook of first love, the she of the eternal broken heart, the she who discovers she is a second wife, the she who is stalked, the she who was once labelled a mistress, the she who carries the stigma of muddled affairs and the unspeakable secrets of errant friends.

I am the woman who does not have to name her lovers, categorize them alphabetically, in the hallowed tradition of a telephone directory. I am the woman not called upon to name herself. I will not face death for denying the details.

I am the woman who will be cursed by society for being passed from man to man to man, hand to hand to hand. I am the woman at whom society cannot spit or throw stones because this me is a she who is made up only of words on a page, and the lines she speaks are those that everyone hears in their own voice.

I am the woman men will not take home to their mother. I am the woman who does not smile about washing-up liquid, the woman who does not reach climax over liquid laundry detergent. I am the woman who, having cooked five-course meals and scrubbed toilets to a shine, publicly despairs about domestic drudgery.

I am the woman who is not a good Hindu girl, a good Tamil girl, a good Kerala girl, a good Indian girl. I am not any of the categories I thought I was, I am not any of the categories I was moulded into being.

I am the woman whose reputation is rusting. Who dissolves her once-upon-a-time in vodka with sliced lime, whole green chillies and sea salt. Who swallows it in the sweet heat of a neat whisky and rolls it into tight joints, smoking it up in circles of regret. I wear it in leopard print. I walk it around in red, outrageous stilettos. I take it to every seedy bar in town. I leave it behind in the beds of men whose names I do not bother to ask.

I am the woman who did not know this woman myself, wild and ecstatic, trapped inside me. She is the stranger I am taking to town. She is the stranger I am getting to know, the rebellious stranger under my skin who refuses to stand to any judgment.

I am the woman with wings, the woman who can fly and fuck at will. I have smuggled this woman out of the oppressive landscape of small-town India. I need to smuggle her out of her history, out of the do's and don'ts for good Indian girls.

I am the woman who is willing to display her scars and put them within exhibition frames. I am the madwoman of moon days. I am the breast-beating woman who howls. I am the woman who wills the skies to weep in my place.

I am the woman who makes sex separate and outside of herself. I am the woman to whom rape has happened, the she who seeks to sleep on a separate bed, the she whose trust was broken, the she about whom it is easier to speak.

I am the woman who has tried to shield herself from the pain of the first-person singular. I am the woman who tummy-rubs every received taunt so that it can be cajoled into sentences.

I am the woman who stands in place of the woman who loathes to enter this story in any of its narrations – police or procedural, personal or fictional – because that woman has struggled so hard and so long to wriggle out of it – and now, when asked to speak, she would much rather send a substitute. Sharing stories might be catharsis, but to her it is the second, more sophisticated punishment. I am the woman deputed on her behalf.

I am the woman who can be removed from the brutality of the everyday – from its dying grasshoppers and fading flowers and starving children and drowning refugees. I am the woman sheltered within words, the one distanced into a movie running in her mind, the one asked to bear the beatings, the one who endures everything until something snaps so that fate can escape her. I am the woman conjured up to take on the life of a woman afraid of facing her own reality.

I am the woman who asked for tenderness and got raped in return. I am the woman who has done her sentence.

I am the woman who still believes, broken-heartedly, in love.

A List of People You Should Give This Book To

(Annotated with Some Reasons Why)

by Deepa D.

Originally published as a review in *The Wire*

I.

TO JUDGEMENTAL FEMINISTS

In March 2012 I was an audience member at a seminar in New Delhi, listening to a woman blame Meena Kandasamy for 'taking' violence from her husband. Kandasamy's essay describing her survival of and rupture from an abusive rapist husband had been published a week earlier and though her publisher would have preferred it if the focus remained on her books of poetry, the entire discussion remained focussed on her personal life – the excitement of these salacious 'revelations'.

Astoundingly, it seemed many of the women in an elite feminist publisher's seminar room had never encountered a woman who had been hit by a husband. Now that they had, some were falling over to distance themselves by victim-blaming. 'That would never happen to me, I wouldn't let it,' as the anthem of the Smug Privileged goes.

The triumph of Kandasamy's book is that is straps you into your seat and makes you ride the rollercoaster for yourself so that you are jolted out of any pity or derision you may feel and shaken into a sense of genuine empathy. Every stupid, horrific question of 'why didn't you' and 'why did you' is efficiently invoked and comprehensively slain and feminism modelled as a way to stay breathing in the face of patriarchal dehumanisation. Unlike the blog posts and comic gifs you may have ignored at your peril, this book shows far more than it tells. After reading it, you really have no excuse for not getting it.

II.
TO LITERATURE PROFESSORS AND CRITICS

True story: Marlon Brando raped his co-actor with his director Bernardo Bertolucci's enthusiastic approval because they wanted her filmed reaction to be real. Women, you see, can't be trusted to make Art: to perform or write or paint informed by their life experiences but in control of their narratives. The patriarchy will tell you that F. Scott Fitzgerald made Art even though the words he plagiarised from his wife's diaries and conversations were called 'crazy' by the same husband who systematically plotted how get her institutionalised. Women's writing, they theorise, bleeds spontaneously on the page like uncontrollable menstruation, a horrific by-product of the trauma that happens to us. There is no craft to it.

When you read this book, watch the ferocity of craft at work. Not just the beauty of the prose—as much an entry fee demanded of women writers as well-formed breasts on women who are actors—but the labour that the structure of the book performs. Kandasamy performs no sleight-of-hand, no plot twist; she tells you unflinchingly what she is going to do to tell this story, and why, and then she does it (sometimes this order of storytelling is reversed).

And so you have Kandasamy as cinematographer, escaping to ceilings to demonstrate how detachment functions as survival technique. Kandasamy as humourist, with a list of parental reactions that begins as comedy in the first chapter, returns the second time as tragedy and by the end is the farce that is often the only way to forgive the sins of those who love and wound you. Kandasamy as Socratic dialogist, deftly wielding the male lovers and abusers to construct meditations on the nature of fragile, violent masculinity. Dr. Kandasamy the socio-linguist, turning scholarship into a pick-axe to excavate the etymology of verbal violence. Kandasamy the dramaturgist, breaking down how the stories of marital abuse are framed and who those framings exonerate, and who they trap.

Most of all, you have Kandasamy the writer who creates male characters with the tantalising artistry of a pastry chef. One moment the husband is a buffoonish maggot, the next a mesmerising duellist, and even as she reduces him to the place that boring archetypes of bog-standard violence belong to, she never minimises the volume of the violence itself. Male writers who set out to portray the Women They Have Loved and Been Hurt By fail at the job so consistently that there are entire libraries of women's studies theses on the subject. But Kandasamy joins the roster of those who can provide a clear-sighted, vivid portrait of modern maleness even as they are Writing While Female. (Did you notice the epigraphs preceding each chapter are all by women who have written about violence? Please notice.)

III.

TO WOMEN WHO HAVE ESCAPED OR THOSE WHO
NEED TO KNOW THEY HAVE A RIGHT TO

This is such a kind book to us. Kandasamy's affectionate concern for her fellow survivors triumphs over any editorial demands of explicit sensationalism. Trigger warnings are folded in gently at the beginning; I was married to a rapist, he beat me, I left and am living still. This is not the kind of binary story that says the only acceptable survival is escape or death—every tiny rebellion, every pragmatic compromise is documented, meticulously, as the victory it is. Kandasamy understands that winning sometimes looks like just coping. There is more time devoted to internal conversations with imaginary lovers than to cataloguing for voyeurs the exact measurements and tints of bruises left. As any well-behaved monster, the husband's violence is not antagonistic as much as obstacle; like dragons or thunderstorms, his role is merely to forward the hero's journey. And Kandasamy's hero does not journey in a tidy three act plot, at the end standing sticky with the blood of the villain spurting like triumphant semen. No, instead her journey is a gathering of selfhood, basket-weaving together memory and philosophy, strategy and sensation, to construct her body into what Ursula Le Guin describes as 'the tool that brings energy home.'

TO POETS WHO ASPIRE TO WRITE

Kandasamy is so sharp and so playful that you can watch her flip like an acrobat from satire to pathos without letting go of your hand. She has a gift for conveying theory in vivid images that make it stick. It is so much fun to understand the complex thoughts that she gift-wraps in the simplicity of verbal imagery.

On classical Tamil: 'Keep in mind that this is a language where the word for obstinacy is also the word for intercourse.'

On culinary choices: 'Every day I serve food to him as if it were a declaration of chastity.'

On friendships: 'It is the easy way women dress and undress in front of each other, our clothes made for the hands of our friends, the zip that runs along the length of the dress, the bra hook, the sari pleats at the back, as if we become complete only when we take part in dressing each other.'

On bachelor politicians: 'This label conveys that he takes his semen seriously.'

On lovers (desi version): 'Some men leave me even as they are with me, knowing that I will never be able to love them the way their mothers loved them, and that they will never be able to love me the way they love themselves.'

On lovers (phoren version): 'Here, I do not have a lover to whom I can write poems about the rain. Here, the rain itself is a nice stranger I do not want to know, not the intimate monsoon showers of home.'

V.
TO YOUNG GIRLS CONTEMPLATING LOVE AND MARRIAGE

There will probably be some stodgy serious uncles who think this book can serve as a cautionary tale on the dangers of love-marriage, but if their mistake serves to get this book in the hands of young ladies who are reading romance novels for the porn, then more power to them. Because this is a book about love and sex as much as it is about how men can misuse both to perpetuate abuse and we are very lucky that it is. Because Kandasamy can write about the cunt not just as tragic victim of vicious insult, but as the moist, eager seat of the mathanapeetam (the yonilingam, the clitoris). She can write about men's bodies as objects of desire, not just as weapons. So much of male-written literature conceives of peace, for a woman, as freedom from sex. Kandasamy's book knows better. Men are hindrances or helpers towards sexual play, but peace is the state of being able to choose the sexual self, again and again. She knows that the happy ending is not a lover (though if you want it go look at the dedication) but the freedom to love. There is brutal honesty in her documentation of lovers and her own compromises and missteps in her interactions with them, but it is not truth-telling with the derision of the recently-converted towards former hedonism. In creating a space to perform fragility, Kandasamy reveals strength in choreography similar to a padam where the lover has not changed from beginning to end, but we have witnessed something unique about a woman in love.

VI.

TO PARENTS, MENTORS, GOSSIP-MONGERS AND
SUNDRY GATEKEEPERS OF MORALITY

The feminist movements have fought for words; creating taxonomies of abuse because the act of naming and classifying leads the way to resisting. You can find succinct and revelatory blog posts and essays on the subjects within this book; gaslighting, cycles of abuse, victim-blaming, trapping FOG (Fear, Obligation or Guilt) and emotional blackmail, slut shaming, reproductive violence, toxic masculinity (I could go on for a while). But we invented stories for a reason, because a tale helps make education more palatable than a lecture.

'But is it fictitious?' you ask.

Oh, hush.

She tells you the reasons it must be called a novel.

Read carefully.

Structurally: it makes perfect sense to reduce a violent nuisance of a man into a story; a fiction that permits an author to trap him in the chronological metre of the poetry she chooses and so that we are all spared the nonsense of 'but I didn't hit her with a Mac power cord, it was a PC!'

Pragmatically: it is legally dangerous to talk publicly about cases that are sub judice.

Philosophically: 'Sharing stories might be catharsis, but to her it is the second, more sophisticated punishment. I am the woman deputed on her behalf.'

VII.
TO MEN, WHO MAYBE HIT THEIR WIVES

You can give the book as a warning, I guess, to men you suspect are abusive, as an 'I've got my eye on you' message. It might work; fear of social censure is one known way that domestic abuse can be prevented. But the book's job isn't to reform abusers; anyone awful enough to be one in the first place will walk away from the book going, 'Well, I don't step on her face so I'm nothing like him' or 'I never deleted all her emails so this doesn't apply to me.'

No, the book's job is to remind men that they should know their place, and in the fraught, perilous world of domestic abuse, theirs is tertiary. The story of marital violence belongs to the women who survive it, the families and friends who support them and the nuance and complexity of the personalities recovering in healing from its trauma. Kandasamy creates a male character who can and does claim every special snowflake backstory—abusive childhood, state persecution, military trauma, a poet's sensitivity. And in the end it matters not a whit because he crumbles to dust like any replaceable oppressor who made a choice to participate in dehumanising someone. It may be his words as the title of the book but it is her story and she has cut him down and out and through; appropriating his violences for her profession as a writer. The book, as they say, does what it says on the tin.

Get it?

No? Not yet?

Then add one more to the list –

VIII.
YOU (BECAUSE YOU NEED TO GET IT OR BECAUSE YOU NEED TO KNOW SOMEONE ELSE GETS IT TOO)

Like climate change, domestic abuse is pervasive, inescapable and universal. Either you know what it's like to have a home become unsafe, or you know someone who does, or you're part of the problem with your ignorance that disinvites confidence sharing. If the latter, this book can teach you without perpetuating the hurt you would cause if you asked a survivor in the flesh to testify in the court of your uninformed opinion.

If the former… you don't have to read it, certainly not, and do what you need to avoid being triggered. But, I suspect, you will want to. The sorority of survivors can be a lonely one. It is good to hear from one of us whose words were strong enough to carry her out.